Dancing with Fate

Book Two

A Queen

For

Her Enemies

F. J. NAMINI

F. J. Namini

The official website of F. J. NAMINI

https://fjnamini.com

Contents

CHAPTER ONE

EMBRACE THE FIRE

Ancient Land of Mannea, 627 BC, summer

No," Mithra said from between white lips, grabbing the horse rein. "No, no, no."

Astyages caught her wrist. "Mithra, it's too late! We need to go as far as we can into the forest," he glanced up through the mountain. "They are Bannermen warriors; I know they don't come without a troop behind them."

"Are you listening to what you're saying?" Mithra yelled at him.

"You know that you can't save her," Astyages said, trying to stay calm.

"I only know that she's my mother!" She yelled as tears blurred her vision. "I've nursed to sleep on this voice, the same voice that is crying out for help now..." A lump in her throat choking off her words. She brushed away unfallen tears with the back of her hand, she slammed her heels into her courser's flank, and she flew through piles of dry leaves that flurried and flew when her horse galloped past.

*****

Brazen was marching north into the mountain. The Assyrians bloody red banner streamed above his head, from his silver lance, shivering and twisting as the wind gusted. Two warriors were following close behind him, screaming some wordless battle cry. They dragged forth Jamaspa's broken body with her hands bound by a rope. The other end of the rope was looped about the saddle horn of Brazen's courser. The men were screaming and cheering, so entertained ourselves with their wild game that did not see Mithra's coming until she approached them.

Brazen threw a glance back over his shoulders, put his heels into his courser and galloped ahead, toward a large hill's top in the distance. Others slowed and stopped. Mithra saw nothing except her nanny's bloody body, tried to reach her. She did not even notice that one warrior drew his sword, galloping toward her and began to scream but at the same time one arrow took the warrior in the throat, stopped his screaming. He fell from the saddle. Mithra caught one glimpse of the man's startled face as the bright blood came rushing out his throat, then glanced back over her shoulder, Astyages was coming after her to attack the second warrior.

Mithra leaned forward in the saddle and urged the horse to a gallop. "Faster," she told her horse. "You can, you can."

Brazen was riding up the hill, Mithra following him, a tiny distance behind. Morvarid was galloping like the wind, Mithra's cheeks were ruddy with the cold wind, but she ignored them and drew her dagger. "I will cut the rope in two seconds if you take one more step," she murmured, as collapsed facedown on the

2

saddle, saw sparks fly underneath his horse hooves. That's the final step, she thought as her blade sheared the rope in two and Jamaspa's bloody body left behind.

Brazen howled in fury as he watched Mithra, beside himself, staring at him with her beautiful burning eyes. Both horses were lathered. Brazen came beside her, flew at her like an arrow, knocking Mithra down to the ground, both rolling when they landed. Brazen, leaping like a panther landed on Mithra's chest and seized her arms, trapping them to her side. Mithra struggled against him, shooting her legs out but her movements were far too slow. She gave him a sharp poke in the face with her head knocked him backward and dragged herself from beneath his body. Brazen whirled, cursing, caught her foot and sent her plunging to the ground.

Slowly, Mithra tried to get up but sharp pain lanced through her head. Brazen got to his feet, moved a foot and knelt beside her, so they were face-to-face, held her tight by the hair. He smiled and raised his dagger to the sky. Mithra has raised her face, stared him with large, honey brown and unafraid eyes, waiting for him to slit her throat but Brazen was too stunned to move. He knew this girl's face very well, these beautiful eyes, and this birthmark on her face, a sign like the shape of a skull, was so familiar to him! This is just a nightmare; a voice inside him whispered and lowered his hand. An inch. Another. "You... you are..."

Jamaspa's hands closed around his throat before he had the chance to finish his words, hard as stone, choking him. "Don't touch my daughter, you filthy vermin!" Jamaspa shouted, her fingers pinching in Brazen's neck firmly. Brazen's left hand pin his attacker's left hand as he turned and stabbed his dagger in Jamaspa's chest. Jamaspa sighed; her frail body almost fell on him as her fingers loosened. Brazen's hands grabbed hold of her shoulders to shove her away and snatched up his dagger, coughing.

Mithra's eyes gaped wide and crawled toward her nanny's body, screaming with every step. She fell on her neck. "No, no, no, no...," she whispered, weeping. "Please... Don't leave me, please."

Jamaspa stared at Mithra's eyes, offered her last look to her, fully love, a faint smile playing about Jamaspa's deformed lips and closed her eyes, forever.

"You saved my life, for the second time!" A tear ran down Mithra's cheek. "I love you!" She said a sentence that she had never told her nanny when she was alive, her voice breaking. Her fingers tightened into fists, her nails digging into her palms, and turned to Brazen who could not stop staring at her, aghast. She was ready to attack, but an arrow landed on his throat and opened it. Brazen's heavy body fell down by the shot.

Astyages lowered the bow, "Goddamn son of a bitch!" He muttered, low under his breath and stepped up beside Mithra. He stared at Jamaspa's disfigured face with her smile, glistening on her lips yet. "This is the most beautiful face that I've ever seen," he said, sadly.

Far off to the north he heard the sound of horses' hooves and shouting. *The Assyrians,* he thought anxiously. The steep slopes sudden covered with warriors, marching. Astyages grasped Mithra's arm. "We need to get out of here, come on, now!" He said, growing frantic. Mithra threw the last glance at her nanny as Astyages dragged her beside their horses. Astyages climbed onto the horse. "Go through the woods!" He said as he put his heels into his horse and trotted away.

Mithra knew these woods better than everyone. She could lose Assyrians in thick woods trails and wild rivers easily, but the forest seemed ominous far and unreachable. She could hear the clatter of their hooves on the rocks, faster than before. She had no time to glance behind her, but she saw Astyages from the corner of her eye, coming after her. Morvarid, as if she had sensed the danger, was galloping like wind and soon she was several steps ahead of Astyages. The remaining distance seemed endless. Mithra was struggling to breathe despite the wind that was rushing to her face and her terrible pounding heart that she was feeling in her chest.

"We can do it, we can do it, we can...," she repeated over and over.

It was a relief when Mithra saw oaks trees, armored in grey-green needles. *It isn't much farther now,* she thought. She glanced back, Astyages followed close behind her, but Assyrians warriors were seen in a cloud of dust coming far away. It sounds like they were getting away from Assyrians but suddenly a glint, lit by the evening sun, drew her attention. A spear came hurtling from the shadows behind, Astyages must have been the target, but it was his horse that was hit. The spearhead went in its back, the animal screamed and collapsed. His horse fell, snorting blood and biting with his last red breath. The world throbbed, Astyages rolled onto his side and pain shuddered through him. Mithra brought up the rear, Morvarid stood up on two legs, the sound of the whicker mingled with the screams. She stared at Astyages, the blood rising to his face; still, his eyes did not seem to see anything but Mithra.

"Go Mithra! You must go away as faster as you can, go!" He was pleading. "Go, please!"

What is he talking about? He obviously lost his mind! Whom can I leave half of me? Mithra thought. She turned Morvarid's head toward him, oblivious to her anxiously sniffing at the air. Her

5

blood was roaring in her ears. She grabbed Astyages by the hand and pulled him to his feet as the warriors raced ahead. Mithra raised her eyes and saw them, near enough to see sunlight glinting off their horned bronze helmets, there was no chance to flee. The Assyrian warriors surrounded them, howling. A raven croaked from the nearby oaks, and Mithra heard the sound of wings as the black birds flying.

"No," Mithra said, moving a hand to the hilt of the long dagger she wore. "I can't be their captive!"

"Wait, wait, you don't want to fight them!" Astyages said with anxiety. "This is crazy!"

She glanced at him, her red lips curled in a faint, sad smile as she clasped the hilt of the dagger. "I don't intend to win," she raised it high.

The warriors stepped forward, raised their swords, ready to attack.

"Don't do anything stupid, we'll run away together," he promised as prepared himself to defend her if necessary. "Put the fucking dagger down, now!"

"Do you honestly think you can get away? This is an illusion, young commander!" A familiar voice said.

The soldiers made way as Saber rode past. He wore a purple cloak over an embroidered tunic, like an Assyrian commander. "They get you to Nineveh, my prince! A place that many of you have never heard of, probably," his wide mouth twisted in a mocking grin. "They say, Nineveh's gate watch never sleep, they moved faster than the eye could see, they have been underwater for years and don't run out unless by the magic! Running away is fucking impossible!"

Mithra rushed toward him, filled with rage like a battering ram but a warrior reached up and grabbed her by the wrist with one hand. Turning, she glimpsed a robust man with a shaved head and a sunburnt face. She tried to step backward, but the man put his other hand between her shoulder blades, propelling her forcefully toward a trunk, with the other, he wrenched the dagger from her and pressed his sword to her throat.

"Nooooooo!" Astyages shouted as another warrior seized him by the shoulder and hold him forcefully.

"Enough," Saber commanded.

The warrior pushed Mithra down to ground wildly and stepped back obediently.

"I know exactly what's going on in your head...," Saber said sullenly, put his huge hand under her chin and forced her face up. "An honorable death, it is a worthy gift... no, I won't let you have such a blessing." His fingers held her jaw as hard as an iron trap. She had to look. "You have to live an endless existential nightmare, have to keep living, even though this life is horrible."

Mithra had a sick feeling in her gut, but she looked at him straight in the face, trying to hide the fear behind bold eyes.

Saber gave her a long look. "I hate women," he mumbled quietly as if talking to himself. "They're all unworthy bitches," he turned back to her, added, louder. "Oh, by the way, someone is here, someone you're going to find very special."

Saber pointed toward soldiers, at the end of a long rope, Mithra saw Nahira, the rope tight around her neck, her face swollen, with

7

a large bruise on her forehead. Her eyes stared off into the distance, and her face was strangely empty of expression. Mithra could not dare to believe what she was seeing. When she found the courage to move, a few moments had passed. She rushed to Nahira, embraced her head and stroked her long hair, with trembling hand. Her hair was stiff with dried blood, more congealing in her face. For an instant, Saber could see the fear in Mithra's golden eyes, then rage replaced it.

"Only a beast can do it, a devil, like you," Mithra said quietly, a lump in her throat would not let her shout.

Saber raised his eyebrow in surprise. "Me? No, it was not me! I'm not interested in being a part of your family quarrel!" He said as he turned to an Assyrian soldier. "Come forward, don't ever be ashamed of who you are." Saber had a smirk little smile. "Let everyone know, you deserve a better future."

Mithra's eyes turned toward the warrior beside Saber, she recognized her brother even though a little of his face could be seen beneath his helmet. He gazed at Mithra, his dark brown eyes unblinking, expectant, frightened. He raised his hand, slowly and hesitantly, and took his helmet off. Mahbod was dressed in silver armor and purple cloak, and his thin, slender hand held a long sword. His delicate beauty was not fit for a warrior.

"Aren't you ashamed of breathing? You are poisoning the air!" Mithra said with disgust. "How could you? How could you do this to her?"

Mahbod's face looked like a child who wants to find an excuse for his bad behavior. "This is her fault… I had no choice… She tried to escape." His breath frosted the air in small nervous puffs. "I trusted Nahira, and she betrayed me. I…"

Saber made him silent by raising his hand. "No victory is without cost. We have to pass through an unpleasant way to achieve a better future," he said proudly as he looked at Mahbod. "A strong man should be able to overcome his feelings. This is a sign of power and strength."

"I already knew that you want to break the unity of the different ethnic groups of Mannaeans, but you really couldn't find anybody better than Mahbod?" Astyages said, then grinned and added. "You know what; I think you are right, no one is fool enough to believe your bullshits and could even beat an innocent girl from his family brutally because of you!"

Saber glanced at Astyages' flushed and angry face, mocking. "I have no doubt that Mahbod will be a better king for Mannaean people than your insane king with delusions of victory over the Assyrians strong army. We need to stop him before more of our people get killed," He pointing his finger at Astyages in a threatening gesture. "You and your king discard established god's values for achieving fame and popularity."

"Do you really suppose you or your stupid contingency plan will bring the glory to our land, Media?!" Astyages said as he grinned.

Saber threw a hatred glance at him. "All I do is based on my devotion to God, that's what you don't understand!" He said as an Assyrian warrior brought his horse and helped him mount. "Keep your eyes on them, if they get away... I'll skin you like rabbits," he added in Assyrian tongue.

The soldiers tied the rope around their writs, so tight as to cut off the blood to their hands.

"Mahbod! Don't be stupid! Don't lay faith in him." Astyages said, his face was dark with fury. "This bastard will sell his mother for his own benefit." His words frosting in the cold air.

Saber turned his horse's head slowly. Mithra had never seen him so angry before. His small eyes got wide, and his face was as pale as milk. He seemed like a body without a soul, staring at Astyages from the grave. He dismounted slowly, started back the way he had come, his footsteps falling heavily. Mithra's heart trembled in the chest when he saw his eyes glittered with fury. Saber drew a dagger from his belt and held it right under Astyages' chin. He had no intention of Mithra's screams. When he twisted the dagger, a trickle of blood ran down the blade. The dripping blood was the only thing that could finally draw Saber's attention from Astyages' face. His eyes followed the blood, seeping on Astyages' white cloak lined with fox fur. When Saber raised his head, there was no sign of anger in his face, and he looked at Astyages with cold, dismissive eyes.

"I promise you… one day, before too long, you will find yourself wishing that I'd killed you." He smiled, a dangerous smile, added, "Your stupid pride will be crushed beneath slavery in Nineveh." He slipped his dagger back away. "You'll see!"

*****

In the distance a cloud of grey smoke and black dust came billowing up, Dihe was burning from horizon to horizon. In the sky behind the village, the top of Holy Mountain was visible through thick, black clouds of smoke, Immense, forbidding, and safe, where Mithra wished to be there. A massive lump that had formed in her throat was choking her. She looked around.

The Assyrian soldiers settled in the mountain. A few large tents were erected for the chief commanders, a massive fire burning in front of each tent. A large number of people sat on the wet soil, they had taken captives all from the tiny villages located around the mountain. There was no brave warrior, only scared people, mostly women, and children, all men were very old or very young. All captives had been tied by rope.

The sun cast its golden rays down upon the clouds of billowing smoke, turning them bright red, fire red. The rain began again a short time later. It was growing colder. They sat cold and hungry, but the smell of grilling meat on fire seemed disgusting, the Assyrian warriors have stolen their flocks, and their herds, their horses and their cattle, and all things whatsoever did belong unto them. Off in the distance, a wolf howled.

Mithra could hear Astyages' heavy, nervous breathing. No one spoke. From time to time Mithra glanced at Nahira; she was awake, looking into the far, unknown distance. She had threw up yellow bile, twice. She did not complain, did not sleep and did not speak.

A horse reared. Mithra startled by this familiar sound. She turned back sharply, back at camp, a fat Assyrian warrior held Morvarid's bridle while tried to stroke her flowing milk-white mane. Morvarid reared up on two great legs. The man yanked his hand back, muttered a curse, but a smile on his lips showed he had loved this horse. Mithra lowered her face, wiped away her tears on the sleeve of her shirt, furious that she had let them fall, but her soft sobbing betrayed her.

Astyages turned her hand over and lightly kissed her wrist. "Don't be afraid, honey. We'll find a way, okay?" He said.

"This is all my fault. It was my foolishness; otherwise, you wouldn't be here." Mithra muttered under her breath.

"Don't say this. Maybe if I had thought about it, I would have done exactly the same thing." Astyages took a deep breath. "Being here is no one's fault."

"This is my fault!"

Mithra and Astyages stared to Nahira's pale face at once, startled. Her voice was so flat, her face strangely empty of expression, and for a moment they thought maybe... just maybe... they got it wrong, but Nahira continued, "I knew Saber was here... I knew Mahbod meet him in his hiding place... I chased him, I thought there is another woman... when he realized that I knew everything, he made me swear never to tell you... He said Astyages kill him if I spoke, but if I don't talk about it, Saber will help him to be rich and famous. They were just supposed to kill Astyages, that's all. If he had died, I might have married Mahbod." She sighed deep in her chest. "This is my fault!"

"I can not believe what I hear," Mithra said, shocked. "I mean, this whole time you've been helping me to prepare my wedding ceremony, whereas the groom was supposed to be killed." Nahira did not answer. "You're delirious. No?" Mithra said. Nahira stared out to distance, remaining indifferent even.

"Don't make yourself suffer unnecessarily, try to sleep," Astyages said to her with pity in his eyes.

Mithra closed her eyes, hoping to find comfort. "Yes, try to sleep!" She said.

*****

Saber stood outside his tent, staring into the fire.

The tent was warm and airless, and he needed some fresh air. He raised his face, hoping the cold wind from the mountain reduce

12

the hotness that he felt deep inside him. Astyages' words echoed in his mind and hurt him again. It was not the first time in his life he had been humiliated, a cold wind suddenly slapped on his cheek, and his thoughts flashed back to the beginnings of his journey, that seemed like forever ago, the days, which he was not interested in thinking about it… when he was a little boy.

*****

It was cold as ice, and the only sound was the sigh of blowing snow.

His limbs felt stiff and frozen, and his dirty, ragged clothes could not keep him warm. He had been sitting on an overturned barrel for a long time, waiting for his mother. He could hear the singing of his mother, coming from their hut. He wished he could be in there with her mother, but his mother had told him he should get the hell out of their hut while that stranger was there. Their hut was far from the village, and there were no houses around to give him a shelter from the cold burning wind that whipped on his body. The snowfall that blanketed whole the mountain had finally stopped, but it seemed even colder than before. It was a black night, with a full silver moon appearing and disappearing as the clouds blew past. He could see a reddish light shining from the windows of their little hut. The freezing cold wind helped him to forget his mother's warning; he crawled inside the hut, hoping to attract no notice. An unpleasant odor of a stranger's body had filled the hut, but the welcome heat beat against his face as he entered and he decided to sit beside the fire. A bronze wine cup crashed behind him and made him jump and howl.

"Mischievous mice! I've told you, don't fucking move," said his mother, laughing drunkenly.

The man started laughing too. He shoved his whore aside and got to his feet. His sword belt hung on a peg beside him. He was naked, and Saber could see his cock, hard and wet. He lowered his head; his desire for being at home had vanished.

"Little boy-man," the man said as he filled his wine cup again. "You want to stay here, huh? Maybe you would like to see how fast I could fuck your mother! Right?" The man said then gave a bark of laughter.

He was only eight years old, a little boy, but for knowing the humiliation, you do not need to be a grown man. He ran out of the hut. He ran vigorously through a narrow path between rocks, covered his ears with both hands. His breath frosting in the air, heart pounding. He kept running, splashing in the muddy puddle as he did. His rotted felt shoe became wet and heavy, he felt the frozen mud between his toes, and only a few steps further he dropped to his knees. The ground was cold and hard. He took a long breath and began coughing, after a moment he recovered, turned and saw the hut in the far distance. He had just find out he was alone. He looked around, a cold wind was blowing and made the trees rustle like living things, a wolf howled at the moon. He tried to move but suddenly heard the soft crunch of frozen snow crust.

A great shadow emerged from the winding road towards him. "Someone there?" A voice screamed.

He could not answer even if he wanted to, his whole body shaking. He closed his eyes; he was horror-struck. When he found the courage to look again, a long time had passed and he saw the shadow close to him. He swallowed, remembered his mother had told him if he would act like a petulant child, bogeyman would steal his soul and eat his flesh.

14

"Hey, who are you?" The bogeyman said.

The bogeyman could speak, he thought. He could feel the sweat on his skin, despite the cold weather, and the thumping of his heart against his chest. He hugged a big boulder, his nails scrabbling at the stone. He could hear his rapid breathing. Hesitantly, his eyes look at the bogeyman. He expected to see a horrible face, but a man was looking at him with his tiny black eyes. He stared at the man curiously. The man weighed him long and carefully with his eyes.

"You are Silvery's son, Huh?" The man said.

He did not answer.

"Yes, you're Silvery's son, you have gotten her sinister eyes," the man stroked his beard.

"Well, so I'm your father!" He said, his tone was calm, flat, uncaring.

He still stared at the man, shocked.

"What are you looking at me like that for?" The man said. "That bitch never told you that you have a father, huh?"

Saber was speechless. He sometimes had heard his mother curse his father, but she had never told him that he has a father.

"So she never told you! Fucking bitch!" The man muttered. Then he raised his head. "What's your name?"

"Saber," he answered for the first time.

"Why are you wandering in the mountain?"

Saber hesitated for a while. "My mother has a guest!" He finally said timidly.

The man rested his hand on the hilt of his sword, grinned. "Aha, I see!" A gust of wind blew up. Saber shivered violently. "Are you cold, son?" He glanced at his son. "Get up," he screamed at him, opened a woolen shawl from his waist and threw it over Saber's shoulder. The warm shawl gave him a sense of joy. Then the man pulled out a handful of raisins from his pocket. "Raisins," he announced happily.

Saber filled his mouth with raisins hastily. He had eaten no more than half a day past. He wiped his mouth with the back of his hand. It did not matter this man was his father or not, he treated him kindly and did not seem like others.

"Would you like to come with me?" The man said.

Saber nodded happily.

The man stared down at his son and smiled. "Okay, but I am not a patient man, keep that in mind," his father said. "You must do everything I say and learn fast."

"I'll do it!" Saber said.

"Good, but first there's something I have got to finish," his father said and took him by the arm, his fingers squeezing so hard that they hurt. He pushed him through the beaten trail. "Show me the path I must walk!"

They moved up through the narrow and crooked path. The man's feet made no sound as he climbed the hill but Saber was feeling him at behind, he was muttering to himself as he walked and Saber did not dare to look at him. Near the house, he stopped.

"Here!" Saber said as he pointed.

The man drew his sword from its sheath, a long sword, like none that Saber had ever seen, and kicked the door open. They find her mother sleeping, hugged the stranger man tightly to help keep him warm. They wake up scared. His mother made a frightened whispery sound as she looked up at his father and wanted to run away, but his father grabbed her roughly by her long hair. Only a slight movement of his sword was enough to open her white and delicate throat.

The stranger man threw himself from the bed, tried to reach his sword but his father kicked at the sword and sent it skittering across the floor, far from the man's hand and poked him in the gut as he tried to get up. The man sat back down with a grunt. Saber's small eyes widened, his mother lied here dead. His father threw aside the blankets, and her mother's body rolled out of bed and landed on the floor.

"Little bitch, you thought I'm rotting in a dungeon!" His father said in through his clenched teeth. He turned to his son, who was shivering violently, even in the warm room. "The first lesson, never trust women, they are all bitches!" He said firmly.

His father lifted him off the ground with one hand and put him on the bed, besides the bloody sheets. He pointed to the naked man with his sword. "What do we do with him?" His father asked.

Saber had no answer. He had never been so scared in his life; he glanced at the man. The naked man was trembling, his face as pale as the snows outside. He was afraid, but the sight of the man had given him a pleasant strength. This good feeling gradually flowed through his veins. He stuck to his father's body and enjoyed the feeling of being a strong man.

"She... didn't tell me that... she is married... if so... I didn't come here," the man said, brokenly.

"How big a fool are you, when I open your throat with this sword, you'll learn to be a little more careful," his father sneered.

The man swallowed. "I have with me a handful of jewelry; it's yours if you don't kill me."

"That's a great story," he said as he straightened the prongs of his beard with his fingers. "But it'll be all mine when I kill you." He went to the man.

The man dragged himself to the floor. "Wait, wait... wait, wait!" He said frightened. "I am a commander of the army. I can give you a letter; ... with this letter, they will give you a job in the army."

His father crossed his arms and looked at him, studying his face. "That's not a goddamned bad deal!" He said as turned to Saber. "What do you say, boy?"

Saber did not know what to say, so he kept the silence.

"You can go wherever you want, far away from this village. No one knows who you are... You can be rich, they'll give you the fastest horses, and you can make your own house, large and luxurious... a bloody fair deal, don't you think?" The man said.

His father stared at the man. "Do you take me for a fool? If you live, you'll break all your promises. I believe what I see with my own eyes."

"I write the letter and seal it...," the man said, hasty. "... right now, right now."

"Let's do that!" His father said. "Be careful, I can read so don't write bullshits. Hurry!"

The man wrote the letter, sealed it, and gave it to his father. His father did not know reading but look at it carefully, then stared at the man; he did not seem to lie to them. He smiled. The stranger smiled too. His father raised the sword and brought it down upon the man.

"The second lesson you should learn, do not trust any man, they all are bastards!" The father said.

*****

The loud sound of a horse's whinny brought him to his senses. A little bit away from the tent, a low-ranked commander held Mithra's horse bridle. Saber glanced at him then turned back to the tent.

Mahbod seemed anxious; he sat silently on the edge of a huge bed that was in the middle of the great tent, fiddled with his cup, looked down at the table where his helmet was. The glow came from the lamp hung over his head, and his brown hair was shining under the flickering light, shadows dancing on his fair skin and showed him more beautiful even though he looked like a child who would burst into tears.

Saber took a step toward him. "What the hell happened to you?"

Mahbod raised his head. "You don't know? Astyages belongs in hell, but they are my family." Mahbod said, his eyes shining with tears. "I'm going to destroy who love me."

There was no affection on Saber's face when he came and sat down beside him. "This is exactly why you should be able to destroy them," he said calmly. "The god can't live in your heart until it belongs to others. The god is looking for men with zeal who are not afraid to prove their power to break the grip of vicious enemies of God. What you're looking for is huge, much bigger than two unworthy women." Saber put a hand on Mahbod's shoulder. "Be a man. Never let a simple fucking woman ruin everything that you've built."

Mahbod reddened, licked his lips nervously and stared at the ground again. Saber got up and walked away from him. There was a way to get Astyages, Mithra, Nahira and everybody else out of their head. He took two cups and filled them with wine. He pulled out a small leather bag from his waist scarf and sprinkled a pinch of fine green powder into their cups.

"Special wine for both of us." Saber said as offered Mahbod the cup. "Empty the cup!"

Mahbod seized the cup. He knew what Saber mean by the word of special wine. He drank and lay back; his cheeks grew warm, flushed. He could feel the relaxing heaviness in his body and closed his eyes, everything changed in a blink of an eye.

Power, pleasure, the whole world actually belonged to him.

Saber stared at Mahbod's delicate face and enjoyed seeing his wicked smile. He drank the wine breathless, threw the cup on the ground and moved forward. He grabbed Mahbod into his arms and took his full lips in his mouth.

*****

She looked queenly, stately in her magnificent bridal costume!

Mithra led the way up the black marble stairs gracefully. *I have climbed these steps a thousand times before,* she thought. Her

20

breasts high and full, her skirt of bloody red silk rode low on her hips and shone with iridescent gold. It was slit up both sides to mid-thigh, flashing a glimpse of her shapely legs with each step. A magnificent ancient palace was in front of her, waiting for its queen. The golden doors opened, and she stepped into the hall. In the black marble hall, the groom was standing, right next to the throne, in a white, embroidered long sleeve robe. She found herself pacing restlessly. She thought for a moment that it was Astyages, and her heart leaped. The groom turned to embrace her. An Assyrian man with Astyages' head in his hands.

Mithra woke with a gasp. She fell asleep on Astyages' shoulder. *Thank God, his head is on his shoulder,* she thought.

"Almost dawn, my love," Astyages said.

The sun was returning to them, and sending bright rays over the stupendous mountain. Mithra blinked toward the sun that brought her a day that she never expected. This day could be so much beautiful if they were not captured. Astyages was looking around anxiously. The soldiers were prowling the mountain like wolves. Their coming and going disturbed Mithra more than she could say, "What the hell is going on in here?"

"It looks like they're getting ready to leave," Astyages said, his voice choked and nervous.

Somehow, everything changed. Every shadow seemed darker, every sound more ominous. The frightened men and women got up, unconsciously jostling for a position, which kept them out of the Assyrian hands, just as we would back away from the edge of a cliff when our instinctive fear sounds the alarm. A dozen Assyrian men were splitting logs to feed the blaze. The echoes of the Assyrian warriors mingled with their shouting. The men spoke their tongue, with words that they could not understand but they did not need to know the words to find out something terrible was going to happen.

A crow was flapping overhead, screaming, Mithra's eyes followed it and took Nahira's arm tightly. For the first time since yesterday, Nahira looked at her. Mithra saw something strange in her eyes, no shadow of fear but … a steady beating drum made Mithra turn her eyes.

Astyages stood and pulled Mithra to her feet beside him.

"Astyages, what's happening?" Mithra asked nervously.

He did not say anything in reply. Suddenly the drummers stopped, and a deep silence descended over the mountain. A silence more horrible than the warriors shouting. No sound had heard but crows screaming and cawing. They all were staring at the soldiers, waiting without a blink. The sound of iron hooves ringing on the rocky mountain, the men and women stare at the passing riders with curious eyes. Five horsemen approached. The dawn light glinting off their spiked bronze horned helmets. Now, Mithra knew two of them well. One of them was Saber when his tiny eyes met hers, his mouth twitched. A young warrior stood behind him, his face beneath the oversized, ill-fitting helm … *my twin brother Mahbod!* Mithra thought in disgust.

The riders stopped, all eyes were fixed on them, the captures and the soldiers. The chief commander, an old man with a grizzled white muzzle and heavily armed, looked at the great pyramid of fire. "We don't have much time, I don't want to give Mannaean soldiers enough time to be prepared to attack us," he said. "The children, the wounded, the old people, whoever can't walk fast, separated them from other captives and get rid of them. Hurry it up!"

The fury on Astyages' face turned to horror; he was the only one of the captives who knew what would happen. He glanced at Nahira, held Mithra tightly. "Whatever happens, don't move," he said.

Mithra stared at him; she dared not ask any question.

The drummers began a slow, ominous beat, boom boom boom; the sound seemed to come from everywhere at once. The chief commander rose up his hand slowly, paused, and then brought it down quickly. The soldiers began to run, rushing toward the people, spears in hand like the dust began to swarm all around them. The wailing was coming from everywhere. The women clutched at their children, screeching, "No, no, don't, please, DON'T..."

The Assyrian men threw the captives roughly to the floor, tore the children from their mother's embrace and dragged them to the fire. Mithra was looking around with a puzzled expression as if she was not sure that she was awake. Astyages took her by both hands and held her before him tightly. The smoke, screams, and moans were making her feel faint. There was a child, began to wail, clutching at her mother's ragged cloak. A weeping wounded man screamed as the flames licked up his legs. "... Please... Please..." His pleading dissolved into one long wordless shriek. Mithra could taste the bile in the back of her throat. She covered her ears and pressed her face into Astyages' chest but still the smell of blood, the smell of smoke and the smell of burnt flesh, was unbearable.

She did not open her eyes until she heard the sound of heavy footsteps. *They're coming... they're coming here!* Mithra thought, with a sick sense of helpless terror. She lifted up her eyes. A warrior with pale brown eyes and a bushy red beard grabbed hold of Nahira's rope and bulled a path through them. Mithra tried to reach to Nahira. "No, No, I won't let you," she shouted. Her fingers were digging into Nahira's arm like claws. The warrior growled something to her in the Assyrian's tongue and threw her roughly to the ground, but Mithra was struggling to hold Nahira with her spirit. The man shoved her down when she tried to rise. Mithra was screaming at the top of her lungs, desperately tried to hold Nahira's hand but her fingers slipped on her hand. Astyages rushed towards Mithra, slid one arm around her waist to hold her in place. Mithra felt hot tears on her cheeks. Astyages tried to steady him. She wrenched free of his grip, stayed on her hands and knees, clutching at grass and rocks, breathing hard. She raised her head slowly and looked at Nahira's face. There was no need to drag Nahira to the fire; she was going to the fire eagerly. At the last moment, when her pale white skin reflected the flames, she turned and looked at Mithra; a drop of tear was shining in the corner of her eye.

CHAPTER TWO

FALL TO ZENITH

Ancient Land of Mannaeans, 627 BC, Autumn

Ten days they had been walking, each day had been worse than the day that had come before it. The drums beat a flat, fast cadence as they marched through the mountain pathway nearest the north. Mithra felt cold to the bone, she eyed the sky, the clouds that had been wispy and white that morning were now darker and dense, but a poke with the end of a soldier's whip remembered her that their every footstep should fell on the rocks in harmony with the beats of drums. As the days passed, the leaves were beginning to turn red, yellow, purple, hues, floating gracefully on the soft breeze, though Mithra did not find them attractive despite their lively colors. The only thing that she could feel was humility and grief.

The Assyrian soldier jerked to a sudden halt at the end of the rope, violently, this meant that they decided to make a camp. The rope around her wrists tied her to the second woman in line, a weary woman who could not stand anymore, her knees bent, and she fell, so Mithra had to fall too. The men and women got separated. Mithra had only enough time to exchange a quick look with Astyages before they were marched away, separately. She could see the sadness in his eyes, but he paused long enough to give her a weary smile to encourage her. After that, Mithra made a conscious effort to keep from gazing at him. She cannot stand to see him so humiliated, so desperate. *We doomed to a life of shame!* She thought.

Mithra took off her torn shoes and took her bloody foot in her fist to ease the pain. They made their way north, a twisting stony pathway through the heart of the mountain, seven hundred feet high. The ground was damp and muddy, with rocks and hidden roots to trip them up. Saber and the chief commander were driving hundreds of captives before them to sell in the slave marts on the shores of Nineveh.

Mithra had not slept peacefully at nights, feared to dream. Every time she went to sleep, saw her again… Nahira was going into the fire, silent, without tears, without any resistance, willing to die!

The sound of the wings of birds led her to open her eyes. A few crows were sitting on top of the branches of the tall pines. Mithra turned her head, with a disgusting face and heard a woman's voice.

"No, No, I'm begging you. Leave me alone," a woman shouted, frightened. "I'm not sick. Believe me, I'm not sick."

A soldier was cutting the rope that was tied around the woman's waist, dragged her to the woods. A brunette young woman who had tied up to that woman by rope grabbed the Assyrian soldier's sleeve. She pleaded, cried something up to him as he passed, the words in a tongue that Mithra did not comprehend. It was obvious that she was begging for another woman's life. Mithra hated watching her begging and hated her too. The soldier landed a quick thrust on the young woman's belly and went to the woods, disregarding to the women cries. The woman was wailing much more, her scream only lasted a few moments, and then a sudden silence fell upon the mountains as if nothing happened.

Death was not shocking anymore!

The soldier came back, grabbed the brunette young woman and dragged her toward Mithra; he tied her hands to her.

The young woman sat down heavily on a wet log beside Mithra and said something in the Assyrian's tongue. Mithra glanced over her shoulder at her. "I can't understand a word coming out of your mouth," Mithra said coldly.

"You really don't speak Assyrian?" The young woman asked with surprise.

Mithra stares at her for a moment, without a word.

"I was pretty sure you are from Assyria."

"Take a good look," Mithra said, her eyes brimmed with fury. "I'm a captive like you, from Mannaeans Land."

"Yes… but you look like them," the young women mumbled in wonder.

Mithra glanced at the woman curiously. "How did you learn to speak Assyrian tongue?"

"My father was from Nineveh," she seemed happy to find a subject to talk. "He was the forefather of a mighty nation, a businessman, a very, very serious businessman, who became the biggest merchant in Nineveh. But unlike the others merchants, he was not searching for treasure, he believed trust is more important than money to a merchant, that was the reason why he broke and came here from thirty years ago, …"

"Well, well!" Mithra said acidly, she leaned back against a tree trunk and closed her eyes. "Enough, I got you."

"Would you like to hear my story?" Her smile was more full than before.

"No!" Mithra sighed and closed her eyes again.

The woman paused, then moved closer to Mithra, to shield her from the worst of the wind. A few minutes later, one of the soldiers threw a piece of underdone goat meat before them. The captives barely have enough to eat. One of the captives was always begging for food. Mithra tried to keep from hearing.

The young woman ripped the meat with her teeth, cracked the ribs to suck out the marrow from the bones. Mithra glanced at the young woman, her stomach was a roil, and she knew she could keep none of it down.

"You should be eating it," the young woman said, her mouth was full of almost raw red meat. "You won't survive dear if you don't eat."

"Listen, don't worry about me," Mithra said, gazing sullenly at her.

The young woman finished her food; put aside the bones. She sat on her knees, bowed down and said a silent prayer.

"Hey, what are you doing?" Mithra said when she had to bend because they were tied together by ropes that loop around their wrists.

The young woman sat straight up, looked at Mithra. "Sorry!" She said, embarrassed. "It is my custom to pray after meals, for being grateful for God's blessing!"

"Blessing?" Mithra grinned. "To which blessing are you referring? The life that is waiting for you is hundreds of times worse than death."

The young woman seemed surprised. "What do you know that?"

"You still don't get it, do you?" Her voice was as cold as ice, and the words were mocking. "You are a captive now poor girl, and a horrible fate awaits you. You have to work hard, without any pay, you will struggle all your life to obtain your masters' blessings, you have to do whatever they want, you give birth to babies who don't have a father, they make you feel like trash, you should bow your head in front of any Assyrian, even the lowest of them." Mithra stared at her for a long moment, she smiles, a smile full of tacit knowledge. "Death is the highest blessing for captives like you!"

"Fate?!" The young woman licked her lips and blinked. "Fate is like a small kid."

"What?!" Mithra said surprised.

"Yes, my father always said that the people believe, kids all looking quite similar to their parents but you can teach the kids all the things that you want so that their own parents could not recognize them."

"I don't think that your father has been a captive!" Mithra said with a cruel sneer.

"No, he was a gambler," the girl said, seeming oblivious to Mithra's ironic tone.

"Are you kidding me?" Mithra said. "You've just told me that he was a businessman!"

"I know, but that was before," she said calmly. "He became a successful gambler since came here, that's why he didn't believe in fate."

Mithra laughed, for the first time in these days, she forgot to be sad.

The young woman laughed along with Mithra. "My name is Savrina; what's your name?"

The young woman's hair was a lovely dark brown, the color of fallen leaves browned and sleek with the first rain of autumn, her large liquid brown eyes held intelligence and serenity. Her cheekbones were not exceptionally high, and her nose was a little too long to be perfect, she was nothing like Nahira but her smile that rarely left her face and her eyes that shone like sunshine on water, remembered Nahira.

"Mithra!" She said finally.

*****

Their long journey was reaching its end.

They walked down the stony hill that led to the river. The river was a sleeping snake, lied across the land in smooth, seductive curves, hot in the morning light, chill at nights. Walking through sandy paths could be easier if captives were not tremendously weary.

Mithra wiped the sweat off her forehead. In the blinding light of the afternoon, the river was like a semi-molten mirror. Her heals' skin was dry and cracked, and the scorching sands numbed her feet. At that moment, sitting in a place of deep silence and brooding shadows was the only thing she had ever dreamed of. Savrina was talking, same as always. Mithra did not listen to her, it did not matter what she was talking about, Mithra just needed to hear her lively voice. Savrina was the only symbol of life. Mithra tried to ignore a sticky, dry feeling in her mouth but at the front line, the commanders urged their stallions into a gallop, stirring up clouds of dust just like a storm wind that caused her to cough. As the dust cleared, Mithra could see a large waterfall around the next bend in front.

They were walking since dawn, exhausted and panting. No one dared to stop. Assyrians keep the captives alive to sell them in Nineveh, and those who were healthy might survive, strong men and women, worthy for selling.

The soldiers stopped in front of a beautiful waterfall.

Mithra involuntarily moved forward with a rush of captives to the river, where fell on her hands and knees. She plunged her face into the water, enjoying the feel of cold water on her parched and cracked lips. Then she looked up and saw her. Her face seemed blurred, as Mithra was seeing her through a veil of water. She rubbed her eyes with the back of her hand. When she took a closer look, she was absolutely shocked by what she saw.

There was a big statue above them, a woman with curly hair, and sword in hand. In the top of the cliff was seen a large crow that covered the woman's naked body with its massive wings and below were carved a pile of human skulls that made a platform for her. Mithra was looking at the woman's face curiously, as she felt a chill ran lightly on her core. On the statue's cheek was seen as an image of the human skull, a sign similar to what was on her cheek.

Mithra staggered forward, passed the tired captives, reaching for the statue, as fascinated as she was frightened. Savrina tied her, had to follow her.

"This is a statue of Semiramis," Savrina said.

Mithra turned to her, surprised. "Who's Semiramis?"

"You don't know her?" Savrina said. "She was the greatest queen of Ashur. Assyrian worship her like their Gods." She sat on the edge of a boulder. She looked tired, too thin and pale. "Her mother was a goddess who fell in love with a mortal man, but then the gods learned that she was pregnant! They blamed her for loving an unworthy man. She bore a daughter, Semiramis, but she drowned in the shame of her sin so killed her husband, abandoned her daughter in the mountain and hid in the lake forever. Crows found her, keep her warm with their wings and feed her by letting drops of milk fall their beaks into the baby's mouth. Semiramis had grown up among the crows! And therefore also crow is holy for the Assyrians!"

Mithra could not take her eyes from the statue. "This is a stupid story, how those people really can believe that?" She mumbled, yet she was impressed.

"I believe it is an incredible story, though she is holy and the Assyrians worship her not just because her story, in fact, people love her because of the glory that this woman has brought to them," Savrina said.

"How?" Mithra said, eager to know.

"She was the great king's wife when the king died. She was his heir and successor until her son came of age," Savrina said. "She had considerable influence at the Assyrians court when women were not admitted to positions of authority in the Assyrians Empire. Semiramis is only Assyrian's queen, who lead the kingdom by herself alone and there was no man better than her in all the time. She built Nineveh and brought Medes lands under her yoke." She raised her eyes and glanced at the statue. "I saw some statue of her before, but this is more beautiful than all of them. Look at her face! She has often been described as a wild beauty. Honestly, I think she looks like you, isn't it?"

Yes! Honestly, she looks remarkably like me, Mithra thought fearfully. But why? How is that possible? Mithra went ahead involuntarily. Savrina reluctantly stood up. Semiramis' sculpture was at the top of Mithra's head. Curly hair, prominent species, everything, even the fine line that sometimes, when she was determined to do something, could be seen on the corner of her mouth, everything was like that statue. Mithra felt with a sense of shame, how much she loves this bloodthirsty queen. She reached up to touch the statue. The statue seemed so alive. Mithra could almost feel the warmth of Semiramis' skin on it.

A soldier punched Mithra hard in the chest. Her body was slammed violently onto the ground, forcing the air from her lungs. Mithra glanced warily at the soldier who was standing beside her, his face red with anger. Slaves' dirty hands should not touch the holy statue of Semiramis. The goddess was insulted that he worshiped her, when the warrior raised the whip above his head; overwhelming feelings of worthlessness and anger boiled up inside Mithra and spilled over in a froth of rage. She grabbed the whip when the end of the whip was sharply swung in the air, wrapped around her wrist and pulled it hard. The soldier staggered and almost fell, but he balanced himself and stared at Mithra. She could see the hard glitter in the warrior's eyes as he stared at her. He stepped forward. Mithra stood up, she was ready to defend, but when the warrior raised the blade above his head, Savrina threw herself at the Assyrian warrior's feet and begged for forgiveness.

Savrina was talking endlessly in the Assyrian language. Mithra did not know anything of her words but knew that she was begging to the soldier.

"Do not beg!" Mithra shouted angrily in a loud, deep voice.

Savrina, holding the soldier's legs very tight and begging, did not pay any attention to her.

"I told you don't beg to him." Mithra hesitated until her anger flared. She bent, grabbed Savrina's shirt collar and threw her backward violently, but as they had tied, Mithra fell down beside Savrina. The warrior lowered the sword slowly, giving a derisive smile. Mithra got up, her red face all smeared with dirt. She banged violently on Savrina's chest.

"I told you, do not beg, you are not a dog to beg for forgiveness!" Mithra shouted.

Savrina was staring at her with surprise. "Do you realize what you're saying? The man was so angry about the disrespectful behavior that he wanted to kill you!"

"I just don't see why you need concern about me, huh? I don't want to keep me safe. I don't want to live, do you understand?" Mithra shouted.

Savrina's lips were trembling slightly. "Because you are scared!" She muttered, low under her breath.

Mithra's fury had reached its limit. "Are you telling me I'm a coward?" She made a disgusted sound. "Do you have any idea what courage means? Did you do nothing in your life but blabbering like a fool and begging to survive? You cannot even imagine my courage. How dare you say that?" She roared, her voice thick with irritation.

"My father said living needs more courage than death," Savrina said, her whole body shaking with the sobs. "You don't want to live because you don't dare to start a new life. You're scared. You're scared of moving forward, you don't dare to find a new way. You are scared!" Tears welled in her eyes.

Mithra stared at her and said nothing. The Assyrian's warriors crowded around them; seemed amused by their fighting. Mithra glanced at them, and her glance lingered on Savrina's tears on her face, feel regret. She lowered her head, hoping that her mind would be satisfied with her excuses, but what really pissed her off was, she might be right. The warriors were mocking and pointing at them, the sound of their laughing was echoing in her mind, but suddenly all went sideways. Mithra raised her head, Saber's horse moved toward her at a walk, and she met his gaze, with joy in his eyes. The chief commander's yelling showed them the time to leave had come. Mithra turned her face away and looked out into the horizon where the sun was shining, and captives were going forth. She got up furiously and walked, oblivious to Savrina who was struggling to get off the ground! She threw the last look at the statue of Semiramis as she was passing, which had created all this trouble for her. It was so strange that she would want to touch the statues yet, it was like that it belonged to her, a lost part of her.

Their path continued along the great river. Savrina was silent and Mithra wanted nothing so much as she speaks again but that night passed quietly.

*****

Mithra woke up, without hearing Savrina's voice, unlike the past few days. Savrina was awake, stare to distance, her breath quivered in short, quick gasps every time she inhaled.

The sun had barely risen. "Wake up. Wake up!" The warriors cried, and the captives' faint and tired moans echoed the response. The Assyrian's drum began to boom, they had to continue their journey without anything to eat. Savrina tried to get up, but she sat back down with a grunt. She took a quick peek around nervously, pulled aside ropes and rubbed her ankle so Mithra could see her skin split open in gout of black blood and yellow pus on her skin.

Mithra moved in closer, and her voice changed to worry. "What happened to your ankle?" She said quietly.

Savrina pushed Mithra's hand. "Move! Don't look at me! No one should know it," Savrina said as she was looking at the soldiers fearfully.

Mithra could not move for a long moment, but Savrina's eyes were begging. Mithra stood, staring at her in silence. Savrina rose unsteadily to her feet, started walking. Mithra was walking behind her, watching her every step. She seemed weaker now, sullen, with a weary look in her eyes.

The road seemed endless. In the blinding light of the afternoon, the river was like a semi-molten mirror. Heat rained down on the captives like the breath of hell. Even the birds were silent, and the grass stood still as if too hot to move.

The drops of sweat stung on Mithra's eyes, and she wiped her face with her sleeve. It was hard to believe they were already into the second month of autumn. Mithra glanced at Savrina. She found her duller than before, exhausted and feverish. *This is all my fault,* Mithra thought. Savrina was walking, slowly but firmly. No one can imagine how hard walking must be for her. How could I talk about courage? She felt ashamed of herself when she saw Savrina's courage. She looked up at the sky, wished the sun remembered that should go down.

Mithra tried to walk more slowly, hoping gave less pain to Savrina but an angry soldier pushed her forward, remembered her that she should follow the drummer. She took a deep shuddering breath and looked around and suddenly, on the riverbed stone, along with pleasant greenness of moss that had covered them; she recognized dark green leaves with black streaks. She remembered all those leaves, which her grandfather was pounding and dabbing them to treat the infected wounds on her arm. *Those leaves could save Savrina,* Mithra thought, but they were a few feet away, and there was no way to reach them when the soldiers would not let her leave the captives' line. She glanced at Savrina's grimace of pain. She already saw in imagination Nahira's face as she stepped toward the fire. *I've lost Nahira. I couldn't bear to lose Savrina,* Mithra thought, *I want those damn leaves, at any cost I had to get there.* The captives must keep going and only a limited time had remained for her. Mithra glanced at the leaves again and overcame at her hesitation. She grabbed a soldier's sleeve, "please... water!" She said, pointing her index finger toward the river.

The soldier slipped his arm free violently and pushed her into the captive's line, the force of it sent Mithra stumbling backward into the arms of Savrina. Mithra glanced at Astyages' shocked face but almost immediately rushed the soldier to grab his cloak before he could go away. "Please...."

"What are you doing?" Savrina asked, surprised.

"I'm thirsty...," Mithra said roughly, without looking at her, her eyes fixed firmly on the man, "please...," she said again, her breath was coming fast and short.

The man stared at Mithra, as fascinated as he was angry, her fingers pinching his arm painfully, gazed up at him, with fury in her eyes. She was begging but imperious and frightening. He hesitated, then took her down to the river. The grass on the bank was sun-warmed beneath her feet, and after just a few steps, the water flowed around her ankle, drinking away her body heat. Mithra sat, just for a moment and Savrina found, to her surprise, that she even did not close her lips to water, but when the soldier escorted them to the line, Savrina saw her smile for the first time.

Every minute passed too slowly but finally, the sun went to rest, and the moon took his place as the darkness began to surround them. The captives sat and dropped their tired body on to the yielding sand on the riverbed. Mithra pulled a handful of leaves out of her shirt, put them in her mouth, and chew lustily in front of Savrina's feverish and surprised face. The bitter taste of the leaves in her mouth gave her comfort. She poured it onto a piece of cloth of her shirt that she had torn and bandage Savrina's foot hide from the guards.

"These leaves are a sure cure for your wounds!" Mithra said happily.

"My father said, some people are like coconut, hard on the outside and soft and sweet on the inside!"

Mithra stared at her face, her mouth twisted in suspicion. "What is coconut?"

Savrina rested her head on her shoulder and closed her eyes. "I love you!" She said.

Mithra did not know what to say, so she said nothing, laid her hands on her shoulders, held her.

CHAPTER THREE

NINEVEH

Ancient Land of Mannaeans, 627 BC, Autumn

The gateway to the great wall of Nineveh was a massive stone and mudbrick arch, the stone retaining wall had projecting stone towers spaced every sixty foot. The stone wall and towers were topped by three-step merlons. Beyond the arc stretched the great wall that the Assyrians had built at the height of their glory, a stone roadway wide enough for four carriages to pass abreast.

The captives, who had survived through this long hard journey, leaned to each other and stared at the gateway with cold, dull eyes, so sad, so exhausted, so weak, wondered at the strange fates that had brought them here. "Faster... Faster!" The tired soldiers droved the captives inside with their shouts.

The captives shuffled past Nergal Gate, named for the god Nergal, god of war, flanked by stone sculptures of Lamassu, the huge winged bull-men and entered the noisy city. Nineveh was the largest city that she had ever seen. Mithra thought it must be ten times as large as the Dihe, a vastness without any mountains and hills. *I will miss the beautiful mountains in my land,* she thought.

The broad windswept streets paved in the sand and giant trees were planted along them.

"They are date palm," Savrina said when Mithra held her head up to look at trees, in astonishment.

Mithra paused; gaze out across the city, towers and manses all crowded in on one another, baking in the warm sun. The town looked so ancient and so arrogant.

Sunbaked ferrymen came and went; their naked body was covered only with a cloth that was wrapped around their waist, in bright colors. The men were speaking with shouts in the noise of bustle in the harbor in the Assyrian tongue. The captives had heard that language only from the terrible Assyrian soldiers and now hearing the same dreaded dialect from the skinny men who was running for a living could be strange for them.

The soldiers led them through the grand bazaar, which was flooded, by a sea of people heading in different directions. The higher-class people strutted down the street, wearing silk and satin robes with jeweled belts and flowing sleeves. Whereas the lower class people sat down on the littered floor begging for money. The senior commanders separated their way from them at the beginning of the bazaar and lost from the eyes through the crowded. Mahbod went along with them, during their journey Mithra had seen him a couple of times, each time stranger than before. All senior commanders left them except one, Saber! He had an unfinished job there, and he wanted to complete it.

The captives stood there, the heat was licking at their sunburned faces. They were looking around, confused, hungry, frightened, and numb. Some of the merchants, who had stalled in the old city market, came closer to take a good long look at the captives.

In a cushioned alcove, a fat man with a forked black beard narrowed his eyes. He got up heavily and stepped forward. He had worn a brocade dress and had a thick gold chain on his neck; it seemed he could walk hardly under this lot of gold. He went through the captives, looking carefully at every face. He cupped a man's face in his hands, examined him, and then he shook his head and gave a despairing groan. "Who's buying it? You can't expect me to pay for these skinny sick captives!" The fat man said to Saber. "You should have cared for them better than this Lord Commander!"

Saber grinned. "Have you ever bought a fat and healthy slave? Just name your price!" He said.

The fat man was still shaking his head. "Whatever I'd say, I'll waste my money. They're useless, especially the women," he said.

Saber slid from his saddle. He slowly moved forward, stood beside Mithra and looked at her, long and meaningful. "What are you saying, old man? Look at this young woman! She is strong as a horse." He put his dagger's hilt under her chin violently and lifted her head, so she had to look up into his eyes. "Look! Look how pretty she is! Take her for yourself," Saber said regardless Astyages' angrily shouts.

Savrina grabbed Mithra's wrist firmly. Mithra was frozen by fear; they were talking in a language that she did not know, but their behavior was showing what they were saying. Mithra wrenched her face free. Saber cut the rope of Mithra's hand and separated her from Savrina violently. A soldier dragged Mithra to a wooden beam in the middle of the square, on an elevated platform and tied her to the pole.

"Step forward, Lord! Come, have a closer look! You can't give up on this beautiful girl!" Saber said.

The fat man moved forward, Mithra was taller than him, and he had to raise his face. Mithra stared at him, breathing hard. The fat man smiled with satisfaction and stretched out his hand to touch her face, but suddenly Mithra butted him with her head and broke his nose. The man fell back a step and cried out in pain.

"Fucking stupid bitch!" The fat man shouted as he had taken his nose in hand. "You nearly got me killed Lord Commander! Damn you and your useless slaves. Send them for hard labor, nobody buys them anymore."

Saber came forward with fury. "Let me show you how you can tame her," he said as his dagger's halt raised and fell. Mithra's head hung on her chest with a slight moan, blood was pouring out of the corner of her forehead. "You're seriously afraid of a woman, huh?" Saber said. "Whip her a few days; you will see how she becomes obedient."

The fat man was still staring at him with cold suspicion. Saber looked at him, grew bored, so ripped open Mithra's collar, exposing her breasts, bare, vulnerable. The fat man looked at her beautiful firm breast, smiled and stepped forward but immediately came back with horror.

"What kind of game are you playing here Commander?" the fat man said and took a hasty step backward. "This necklace is from the crown jewels!"

Saber looked at Mithra's necklace, a tablet that was drawn a double-headed crow on it with the red jewel eyes. *Not now, Gods damned, not NOW!* Saber thought. He tore off the necklace from Mithra's neck and took it in his hand.

"What's wrong with you? She must've stolen that!" Saber barked, but the fat man hesitated and stared at him. *This guy is too rattled to do that,* Saber thought. "I want to sell this young healthy girl for three coins! Who wants her?" He groaned in a disgusted tone as he turned to others.

"Wait, Lord Commander! Don't sell your slaves for cheap!"

A delicate woman's voice was heard from behind the people. Everybody looked back and went away with respect, and from a litter, which had halted in the bazaar square, a petite woman let one of her stout black slaves help her down. Her beautiful black long dress had covered her too tiny body and the big jeweled gold bracelets on her hand were highly inappropriate with her spindly hands. A few golden chains that ran in her brown hair could almost hide her many silver hairs, but still some wrinkles around her eyes and two fine lines on the corners of her thin lips showed her older than what she really was. The woman came forward courtly. Her eyes were as black as her robes, full of wisdom. She took her hand against Saber. Saber gave her a long, chilling look. A royal family jeweled sign, something like Mithra's necklace, was shining on her chest. He put the necklace in her hand reluctantly, and the woman locked it tight between her long, thin fingers. Saber could see the smallest hint of a smile playing around her thin lips as she went to Mithra, put her hand fan under her chin and lifted her head. She stared at Mithra's face, weighed her long and carefully with her eyes, and then pointed to the soldier who was with her. He ran, cut the ropes and took her in his arms to the litter. Mithra's eyes were closed, and she was unconscious, flopping like a woolen doll.

"I have not seen you ever Lord Commander, but I suppose you know that the royal family does not pay for slaves. Isn't it?" The woman said with a tint of a mischievous smile.

Saber's mouth tightened in anger even though bowed his head. "I know about the laws, my Lady." He got no response but a scornful silence.

The woman went to the litter. Saber gave a short bow reluctantly to her as his cold look was escorting her. The people parted respectfully to make way for her. At the last moment, Savrina used the guards' negligence and ran to the woman.

"I beg you, my Lady, take me with you," Savrina said.

The woman threw a humiliating look at her and walked again.

"She doesn't know your language; you can't talk to her without me!" Savrina shouted as a soldier reached out for her hand, grasped it, and held it tightly.

The woman hesitated for a moment, "Take this girl into my litter... tie her hands from the back...," she said to the soldier, pointing at Mithra with her head. "... and took this one with yourself!" She stood there, waiting for the soldier to finish work, a voice drew her attention.

"Where are you taking her?"

She turned to the voice. A handsome young man, among the captives, was waiting for her response. His clothes were torn, and his face was dirty, but he did not like other captives, in the young man's eyes concern was weaving.

"Where she should be, Lady Yafa's palace." Her eyes lingered on Astyages' face as if she has the ability to search his heart and mind. "It's a good place, you should worry about yourself because all men are going to the labor camp of Nineveh!" She said before she mounted on the litter.

She kicked on the back of his men with her delicate hand fan, and they started to go.

*****

44

Hara was studying Mithra's face as her litter swayed along curtains were drawn tight. This stranger's face was so familiar to her. *Familiar yet disgusting!* Hara thought.

The noises had faded to a faint distant shouting. Hara turned her face away from Mithra, chewing her lips. This delicate and beautiful face reminded her bitterest memories, too bitter, bitter than she could wipe them from her mind. *Many years have passed from those days but some old wounds never truly heal,* Hara thought. She always asked from the gods to let her avenge her lost youth from Amitira, and now fate had played in such a way that Hara's wish became true.

Her spirit wished to laugh, hardly but instead she felt anger, regret and missing tears in her eyes.

The day was warm and cloudless, the sky a deep blue. The air was rich with the smells of earth and grass. Beyond the city, many palaces had been raised beside the river, with a shining dome, the great gateways in silver and gold, and the banners snapping in the wind with their custom family crest. *Lady Amitira had liked this place,* she thought, looked at Mithra again, *I don't know how she's going to take it.* Almost an hour had passed before the litter swayed to a stop. Mithra waked up with the sudden movement of litter. She opened her eyes with hands tied behind her. The blood that had poured from her forehead, dried on her eyes so she could hardly see. The last image that she could remember was Saber's dagger that was landing on her head, but she did not know where she was now. She looked around and saw Hara, that took her by surprise, and she drew back slightly.

Hara tried to make a smile, but this young woman was watching her with her large, golden, and proud eyes... it was likely they had gone back in time, to years ago. Hara turned away from her quickly and stepped out in front of the marble steps of a vast palace.

"Take her to marble hall," Hara ordered the guard who had stopped beside them.

The guard took Mithra's hand and pulled her out of the litter. They followed Hara. Mithra was looking around in surprise. There was a garden, bright and airy, where tall palm spread dappled shadows across small creeks, which were running through the yard, three peacocks were walking coquetry, and the air was full with the scent of frangipani.

At the threshold, two giant statues were seen, with the human body and a crow's head, likely, they were staring at them, then Mithra escorted across the entry hall, where the mosaic and strips of gold depicted the overlapping circles those had made figure forms a flower-like pattern. Hara went directly to a room. She opened a yellowish-brown bronze door, pointed with her head and the soldier pushed Mithra into the room. Hara glanced at her; her hands and feet were tied. She closed the door behind her. "Watch her well!" She said to the guard.

Hara knew where Yaafa would be at this time of day. Yaafa was spending Nineveh's hot middays at the palace porch, which looked at the river where the cool breeze was blowing from the river at this time of year. Hara clattered up the steps, strode the length of the hall, her leather wooden clogs ringing on the stone, threw open the door without knocking and came face-to-face with a tall, half-naked man with the kind of face that stopped you in your tracks.

Yaafa was reclining on a pile of cushions, beneath a crimson canopy. Her feet were bare, her warm red hair artfully tousled, her robe a samite as green as her eyes. The silk strap of her dress had been slipping over her shoulder, and her open-collar had revealed a part of her breast's olive skin. The golden straps had woven with her hair, and with every move that she made to her head, very subtle and delicately, her emerald earrings that were a perfect match for the green of her eyes shivered.

A very young man, almost eighteen, who had sat on the floor in front of Yaafa, picked up a cluster of large red grapes from a tray of fresh bread, with butter, honey, and fruit, plucked a berry of it and put it in Yaafa's mouth, whispering in her ear.

Another young man went and sat on the bed next to Yaafa's legs. He played the silver bovine lyre, richly decorated with gold, and lapis lazuli. He was also very young, no beard, his coal-black eyes, making look bigger with kohl, had pinned to another young man with jealousy. Yaafa listened to the boy's words and gave a bark of laughter. Hara hesitated half a heartbeat, then rushed into the porch, and brushed aside the silk veil.

"Enough young men, I really need to talk to your lady," Hara said.

The young men looked at Yaafa. She nodded with a sullen face, and the men left them there, one of them happy for Hara's showing up on time, and others, disappointed for her untimely interruption.

"I trust you have an excellent reason for your interruption," Yaafa said as she put her dress strap on her shoulder.

Hara sat beside her on the bed and took the necklace in front of her face. "I think this is a good reason!" She said.

Yaafa sat up straight, shocked and took the necklace in her hand. "Where did you get it?" She asked.

Hara smiled. "If I got this from a girl, a young woman who has come from Mannaeans land... what do you think?"

Yaafa thought for a moment. "If you're thinking what I think you're thinking, then stop thinking, it's impossible, she must've stolen that...," she said with some concern.

Hara interrupted her impatiently. "I'm pretty sure. Assyrians army have captured her in Mannaeans land and brought her here..."

"Just because she is from Mannea doesn't mean she is Amitira's daughter."

"If you come with me to the marble hall, you'll see...," Hara said.

Yaafa tilted her full lips in disgust. "Can't believe you brought her here," she said.

She threw the necklace on the bed, picked up a small mirror with a silver engraved handle from the table and looked at her pretty face.

"Where are you going with all this? You have brought her daughter... daughter of the woman I hate more than anybody in the world! You don't really expect me to be eager to see her daughter, huh?" Yafa said as she was trying to hide a bunch of silver hair that had run through her red hair.

Yaafa placed the mirror on the table and stared at Hara, waiting with an arrogant look on her face.

You are also arrogant and vain, like Amitira, hungry for glory, blind for opportunities, deaf to advise, Hara wanted to shout these words to Yaafa's face but instead smiled. "You need to meet her;

she is a chip off the old block. The girl looks like her mother exactly, or it's better to say, she looks like Semiramis, even more than Amitira because she has gotten the sign which was on Semiramis' face too!" She said.

Yaafa was listening with interest and Hara, who could get her attention, continued. "We can use this girl to our advantage. Semiramis is the Assyrian's goddess, they worship her, imagine, if Sinshar marries with Semiramis's granddaughter, who has gotten her pretty face, no doubt he'll be our most popular heir among the people and let me remind you, we need that popularity more than everything in this world now!"

"Yeah! Yeah! I guess you're right...," Yaafa said thoughtfully, then laughed. "It's ridiculous; I never thought Amitira's daughter would come here to make me the winner of this cold battle!"

Hara stared at Yaafa and smiled thinly. *Finally, everything is going so well,* she thought.

*****

Mithra was sure that she was sold as a slave to this palace. She tried to wipe dried blood from her eyes with her shoulder and noticed her torn shirt collar surprisingly. She looked around. She was in a huge hall, where everything was made of marble, floor, columns, and decoration in the hall had been of black and white marbles that were adorned with sheets of gold. Mithra's eyes remained on a statue of white marble, which was located on high ground. A statue of Semiramis, which looked a lot like the one she had seen, this time decorated with a gold band around her head. The skilled hands that had made that face of the Semiramis was given the attention to all the details, turned-up nose, high cheekbones, and her violent and serious face, all the things that Mithra could see at her face in the mirror.

She took her eyes from the statue. *There's no time to be surprised,* she thought. There was no one else there, and she could get away quickly, so she had not a moment to lose. She bent over, pulling her tied hands down over her butt until they were behind her and ran them under her feet. It was very easy for her, one of the first tricks that she had learned in the cult. She untied her feet first, then tore at the rope on her wrists with her teeth.

She went to the door, opened it slowly. A guard had stood there, leaning on his spear, oblivious to his back. Mithra seized the guard roughly by an elbow and shut his mouth with the other hand to keep him silent. She quickly twisted his neck and yanked the unconscious guard back to his feet, then marched him into the hall. Mithra looked around. There was no one in the vast hall. She looked up the stairs. It did not seem anyone went there too. A light was coming right down the hall, from the colossal yard, where they came from. It was just a hundred yards away. She took a breath to stop her head from spinning and rushed across the hall.

She ran so fast that she was out of breath. I'm almost there, I'm almost there, she repeated again and again to encourage herself, but at the end of the hall, she came face to face with a stout man, which appeared suddenly in front of her. The man was a head taller than the soldiers that were following him, no more than thirty, with copper skin, and red-brown hair, pulling back tightly behind his head and fastened with a gold and ruby holder. His braid was as dark as her hair and heavy with scented oil, waved with tiny gold strains. He had worn nothing but a red silk shawl that had started from his belt, ran on his chest and swung from the back, covered with round golden sheets. His almond honey color eyes looked at Mithra over the top to bottom. Mithra turned away immediately and dashed to the opposite direction, hoping to find a way to escape but only a few steps away, one of two soldiers who was running after her, grabbed her hair and threw her on the floor.

She had lost the chance to escape, and the pain that she felt in her head was less than the pain in her heart. The soldier knelt on the floor beside Mithra; he grabbed her throat tightly and hold a dagger over her face.

"What the fuck are you doing? Would you beat a defenseless woman? Leave her!" The stout man shouted angrily.

The soldier lowered the dagger, stood immediately and bowed his head respectfully. The stout man stepped forward and knelt beside Mithra.

"Are you all right?" He asked.

The girl seemed not to understand him and looked at him with disgust. Sinshar looked down at her, carefully. Her wound had opened again, and he watched the blood run down her pretty face, over her neck, beneath the collar of her shirt and noticed her torn collar that left a part her breast bare. Mithra followed his eyes' direction and hid her breast with her hand.

"Your head is bleeding!" Sinshar said, embarrassed. He did not know why, but he, the great king of Assyrian's firstborn son, in front of this slave girl was too nervous to can hide it. He raised his hand. "Hey, let me see your wound."

Mithra drew her face back from him furiously.

"She doesn't know our language!"

Sinshar heard behind him and turned his head sharply. His mother and aunt were coming down the stairs.

"Who's this girl?" Sinshar asked.

"A stranger who might become a resident in our house!" Yaafa answered.

Sinshar did not notice anything and looked at the girl again, she was thin and pale, it was obvious she was not fed well and did not live in comfort for a long time. He could see the hard glitter in her eyes as she stared at him but after all her face was the most beautiful face that he has ever seen, a face, which seemed strangely familiar to him.

He got up, took Mithra by the arms with tenderness and tried to draw her up but she wrenched herself away from him with unseemly violence. She was not acting like other slaves who were obedient and quiet. Sinshar was more surprised than angry, by the time his mother reached the bottom of the stairs.

"That's fucking weird, I never imagined that I would have to be bear these arrogant eyes once again," Yaafa said.

Sinshar glanced at his mother curiously. Hara opened the marble hall's door hastily, glanced meaningfully at Yaafa and they entered the room. They saw the guard who had woke up, sitting, rubbing his neck, pale and confused. Yaafa looked at Hara with blaming eyes. A soldier came to take out the guard. Hara grabbed Mithra's arm firmly and pushed her into the room.

"How could you leave this wild beast alone?" Yaafa asked angrily.

"Look at those ropes; her hands were tied from behind and her legs too," Hara muttered, low under her breath. A frown of irritation showed between her brows. "I don't know how she opened them."

Yaafa stepped forward, sat on the end of the marble bench sullenly, and reclining on golden satin cushions. "So we may have underestimated this little witch, she has gotten many things from her mother!" She said.

Sinshar sat beside his mother, confused. "Who's this girl?" He was all curiosity. "What's she doing here?"

Yaafa looked at her son with inquiringly; she was in love enough to know the love vibration very well. She turned to Sinshar, put her hand under his chin and forced his face up, her brow creased slightly.

"She's pretty, isn't she?" Yaafa asked.

"Yes," Sinshar wrenched his head and said, frowning. "She is but that's not what I asked you!"

"This beautiful face remind you of anyone, son?" Yaafa said as she smiled thinly.

"Yes, but I don't know where I've seen her before!" Sinshar said thoughtfully.

Yaafa grinned. "You don't know, really?" She said. "So look down at your side!"

Sinshar looked so surprised but obeyed, wordless, and saw the Semiramis' statue then stared at Mithra in stunned disbelief. She was like a living Semiramis, bold eyes, curly hair, beautiful face and even the same sign that was seen on Semiramis' face; this similarity was incredible.

"How is that possible?" Sinshar whispered, astonished.

Yaafa gave her son no answer instead turned to Hara and said, "I just don't know how to talk to her; she will be useless to us without understanding our language."

"There was a girl who knew our language. I've told to bring her …. I supposed she is here now," Hara said.

"What are you waiting for?" Yaafa said impatiently.

Sinshar could see the hard glitter in Hara's eyes, but she left the room without a word, then came back with a young woman a few moments later. Savrina gave a cry of delight, ran closer and hugged Mithra in a bone-crunching hug.

Yaafa waited for a few moments. "Well, enough! Enough!"

Savrina turned to Yaafa and Mithra took her hand firmly.

"So you know our language, huh?" Yaafa said.

"Yes my Lady! I've spent all my childhood in a border village; also my father was from Nineveh so I can speak Assyrian…"

Yaafa interrupted Savrina impatiently. "Enough! We don't sit here to hear your father's story, then stop chattiness!"

"Yes, my Lady!" Savrina said immediately.

"Do you know this girl?" Yaafa asked.

"Yes my Lady, her name is Mithra," Savrina said.

"How do you know her, she was living in your village too?" Yaafa asked.

"No, my Lady, Mithra and I met when we were captives but I know she is the granddaughter of the paramount of a tribe in Manneae," Savrina said.

Yaafa looked at Hara who was chewing her lips unconsciously.

"Ask her, what is her mother's name?" Yaafa said, leaning forward.

"They want to know what your mother's name is," Savrina said to Mithra.

Mithra gave Yaafa a suspicious glance. "Tell them, it's none of their business," she said.

Savrina looked out of the corner of her eye to Yaafa who was waiting for her answer impatiently. "It's better to answer their question, at least we could know their purpose," she said.

Mithra hesitated, their strange behavior had made her curious too, so wanted to know the truth. "Tell them, my mother Amitira and my father Armaz, the senior commander of Mannaean army who bravely fought with the Assyrians and sacrificed himself for his people," she said with a proud tone.

Savrina translated her words into the Assyrian's tongue, fearfully.

Hara looked so pale; a chill went bone-deep when she heard the name of Armaz. She coughed dryly and stared at the garden through the window. Yaafa was restless too. Sinshar seemed was the only one who seemed excited and happy. "So.... she is Amitira's daughter?" He asked.

"Yeah... I guess she is," Yaafa said, pale and confused, then turned to Savrina and said, "Ask her, where's her mother now?"

"I know that her mother has died birthing her," Savrina said.

"Tell her, as she speaks proudly about her father, she should be proud of her mother too, Amitira is the granddaughter of great Semiramis," Hara said, turning away from the window. "Tell her, she is now in the palace of her ancestors, and Lady Yaafa is Amitira's sister."

Savrina looked at her, her eyes widen. She swallowed.

"Didn't you hear what she said? Tell her!" Yaafa growled.

Savrina said to Mithra all she had heard.

"Semiramis... my ancestors!" Mithra said, shaking her head, refusing to believe. Mithra stared at the statue of Semiramis. *Mystery solved,* she thought.

"Tell the servants to prepare a room in the palace for her. Of course, after they bathe her," Yaafa said to Hara.

Hara glanced at her and went to the door, the situation was almost unbearable, and she seemed happy to have the chance to leave.

"Isn't this incredible?" Sinshar said, excited. "I can see only Gods purpose in this poor girl returning to her own home!"

Yaafa glanced at her son with a sly smile. "Do you really think so?"

Sinshar gave his mother a sideways look. "Yeeeeah... but you don't look pleased."

"Yes, I'm pleased, very pleased!" Yaafa said, then turned to Savrina and added, "Tell her, I'm glad she's here."

Savrina told Mithra, and Mithra scowled. She knew Yaafa was lying, she could feel it. Mithra and Yaafa were staring at each other with hatred when Hara came back, she remembered with a grin that she had seen this scene for many times before, but that time Yaafa was much younger, and Amitira was in this girl place.

"I've made arrangements," Hara said as the guards entered into the hall to lead Mithra to her room. "I can see that you guys together brings back so many memories," she added with a grin.

"The old memories!" Yaafa said and stared at yard through the window.

Hara grabbed Savrina's sleeve before leaving the hall and stopped her. "Tell her, it is not possible to escape from here. Around this palace is full of guards. Is that understood?" She said.

Savrina nodded and stepped out of the hall.

"It is unbelievable how Gods have brought my cousin to her land!" Sinshar said again as he still stared at the door, excited.

Yaafa grinned at him. "The gods didn't bring her to our land, the Assyrians soldiers captured her, and it doesn't seem she's pleased of seeing her family," she said.

Sinshar frowned. "The poor girl has endured a lot of hardships on this journey; we should give her time to forget the past," he said.

Yaafa shrugged. "If her attitude was similar to her mother, like her face, I don't think she has the ability to forget," she said then stood up. "Anyway, It doesn't matter. What's important is that we can use it to our advantage. Semiramis popularity will be ours!"

"We must ensure everybody knows that Amitira's daughter and granddaughter of Great Semiramis are here, in the Yaafa's palace." Hara added, "This girl is like a live image of Semiramis. We need only make up her and then she remembered Semiramis to others."

Sinshar stared at them with wonder. "What do you say?" He asked.

Yaafa glanced up at her son. "You need to obtain the support of the people and the courtiers," she said.

Sinshar stood up angrily. "I don't need anyone's support," he shouted. "I still have enough strength to take my right."

"Don't yell silly boy!" Yaafa shouted louder than her son. "The strength and courage are useless against King Etli until you didn't know politics; if you want to rely on the strength of your army, you will be under the Yuk of Etli till the end of your life."

"This isn't politics; this is knavery. You want to abuse your niece to your advantage," Sinshar gave her a sour grin. "That poor girl thinks her family will protect her," he said, his face was dark with fury.

Yaafa stared straight into his eyes. "Politics is a polite word for knavery, and it is bizarre and ridiculous that my son still didn't know that. No matter what this girl think, and no matter what the world thinks, you need this popularity, which you don't have now." She moved forward, stood in front of her son "You have to take what's yours!" She added as she pointed her finger to him. "At any cost, you have to get that damn royal palace!"

Sinshar was panting from anger. He stared at his mother for a few moments. "If I need help, I will ask for it to stay out of my business!" He shouted as he was leaving the room.

The massive bronze door was closed with an awful sound that echoed in the hall.

"How will you tame this young fool?" Hara asked as she was coming forward.

Yaafa smiled. "I know how to tame men, even my stupid son but how do you tame that girl?" She asked.

"Just as all women, with jewelry, beautiful clothes and fear," Hara said.

"I'm afraid you're wrong again, as you were about Armaz," Yaafa said with a grin. "I don't think any of those will be able to tame her. She seems very stubborn."

Hara was coughing, furious of Yaafa's very frankly words. "Maybe I can't tame her with clothes and jewelry, but I know how frightened her," she said as she smiled a small sly smile to herself. *I know your secret, girl,* she thought.

*****

The guards took them to a large room on the second floor. He closed the door behind them, and they heard the sound of dropping clone. Mithra immediately took Savrina's thin fingers.

"Where is Astyages?" She asked.

Savrina looked at Mithra's worried eyes. She did not know how much she knew about the labor camp.

"All the men were taken for the labor camp," Savrina said with some hesitation.

Mithra sighed. "Thank God! So we know where he is," she said and then rushed to the window and stared into the garden.

"Yes, we know, but it's not easy to go to the camp," Savrina said as she was sitting on a large bed with white curtains of silk.

Mithra had no attention to her; she was staring at the beautiful garden that was in front of her. The waterways were drawn on both sides of the garden, and the fountains in the ponds were stroking eyes. Under the coolness in the shade of the tall palms, a few beautiful peacocks were walking with coquetry, but her eyes saw none of those, she just was looking for a way to escape.

"It does not matter. We will find a way to get into the camp… but we must first escape from this place… It doesn't seem so hard," Mithra said finally.

"That thin woman asked me to tell you, there will be no escape from here; the palace guards are watching everywhere!" Savrina said as she was enjoying of caressing the softest pillow that she had ever seen.

Mithra's exploring of the gardens has no result; she pounded her fist against the wall angrily. "Damn! This garden is too big to check the entire," she said. "What? What did you say?"

"I said the thin woman… that one who spoke to you said you could not escape because all the guards are ready," Savrina repeated again calmly.

"Let them be ready, tonight we're away from here," Mithra growled.

"It's not easy to escape!" Savrina said.

Mithra said nothing; she was looking at a soldier who stood under her bedroom's window.

"You're lucky...," Savrina said.

This time, Mithra interrupted her angrily. "It's not luck," she said, she kept her voice low, but Savrina could hear the fury in her tone.

"You come home to your family, and this is your home," Savrina said.

"I'm in my home, into a locked room!" She said with a sour grin. "You won't find any more locked doors here my friend!" She stepped to her. "I don't know why we're here, but I know very well that none of them don't like me."

"All right, well, all right, but now, for whatever reason, you have a shelter, you can...," Savrina could not finish her words.

"No, I can't. I don't want to can," Mithra almost shouted. "I don't want what those people give me as a shelter. Mannea is my home, where the Assyrian's soldiers burned it. I don't want to live in the shelter of those who have taken my shelter from me."

Savrina got up, went to Mithra who wanted to hide her tears from her and grabbed her arms. "I know it's hard, but if you want to escape from this place, your only solution is to be patient," she said.

Mithra tried to wrench her arms but Savrina held her, Mithra could feel her nails digging into her arms.

"You want to get out of here? So you have to know where you're going to go and how you're going to get there. So be wise!" She raised Mithra's arm. "Now, if you want to go out of here, you're going to have to trust me," Savrina said with a faint smile, hoping that would help to calm Mithra. "Now you're in your family's palace. You can be one of the courtiers. You can use their power. The woman who brought you here is an influential woman, she took you out of the slave market, and Saber did not have the strength to resist. You can also use your royal influence. You just have to wait."

"I can't stay here; I can't pretend I'm not the woman I was before. This is not my way Savrina, I can't do that," Mithra said, sobbing.

"My father said when we are not able to change a situation, then is the time to change ourselves," Savrina said. "You have to learn the new ways."

They heard a loud crow voice; Mithra closed her eyes, took a deep breath and nodded.

The opening sound came at the door, loud and unexpected. They turned; an old woman entered the room, two young girls, no more than sixteen were following the woman with baskets of clean white cloths and small bottles of scented oils in their hand. The woman bowed as she looked at their torn clothes up and down, suspiciously, wondering how such a tattered and ragged woman could be a royal lady. They looked more like outlaws. The old woman looked confused for a moment, but finally, Savrina smiled, stepped forward and said, "She is Lady Mithra!"

"You're her maid?" the woman asked.

Savrina hesitated, then nodded slowly. "Yes, I'm her maid." She said.

"It's good. Come with us. You can help me with bathing her and also wash your body," the woman said.

They descended the winding stone steps for a few minutes. At the base of the stairs, the soldier opened a wooden door, which was decorated with sheets of gold in the form of water lilies. They entered, the door locked.

There could see nothing, but the old woman did not need to light, she lit every single oil lantern that was hanging on the walls. In the middle of the great bathhouse, in a red marble bathing pool, water was bubbling out of the ground and waterfalls of warm water were flowing over the bathroom's walls. The girls put baskets on a red marble table with a base that golden branches of lotus had run on it. They stood ready.

The old woman stepped forward with respect. "If you let me, my Lady," she said and raised her head, but felt a sudden shock of recognition. "Amitira?!" She said as she narrowed his eyes. "My eyes grow weaker, is that really you?"

"She is her daughter, Mithra!" Savrina said.

The old woman nodded. "Yes, how silly of me, Amitira could not be so young," she said, as meeting Mithra made her forget all the traditions of the palace. Her wrinkled fingers caressed Mithra's hands. "Your mother grew up in my arms babe. Where is your mother?" She asked.

"Amitira has died at birthing Mithra," Savrina said instead Mithra.

The old woman sighed. "Poor girl, you are as beautiful and lovely as she was," she said then added hastily, "Do you have any news of my lost daughter? Do you know Jamaspa?"

"Jamaspa? ... I don't know this name," Mithra said when Savrina translated those words.

The old woman's eyes shifted to the side and became glazed with a glassy layer of tears. "I'm never going see my daughter again." she forced herself to smile, a sad smile. "Maybe this is what fate desires," she said.

The old woman led Mithra to the pool. She dropped a few drops of scent oil into the water, washed her long, warm red-brown hair and gently combed out the snags. The girls scrubbed her back and her feet. The warm water gave calm to Mithra's tired and wounded body and... she slept.

Mithra dreamt that she was back in Mannea, in her nanny's hut, her head was on Nanny's knee, and she was waving violet flowers among Mithra's hair. Nanny was singing a song, just like when Mithra was a child. *Such a sad song,* Mithra thought. Mithra could not understand a word, but she loved it. Nanny was whispering it with love, and although her stuck lips did not let her have a sweet voice, Mithra enjoyed it.

Mithra opened her eyes. She did not sleep, but Nannie's beautiful song was heard, and her eyes were staring at her kindly. She rushed to get up.

The old woman stopped singing when she saw Mithra's worried face. Savrina sat in a corner, enjoying hot water and whispering the song to herself. She raised her head and looked at Mithra.

"Ask her, where did she learn this song?" Mithra said.

"It's an old Assyrian's song, everyone here knows that," Savrina said, confused.

"Ask her, where she learned this song," Mithra shouted.

"I know this song since I was a child," the old woman said, her voice full of wonder. "I've learned this from my mother, and I taught my daughters."

"Yeah... Jamaspa knew that, too!" Mithra said with tears.

The old woman was staring at her in silence. Mithra put her head on her knees. "Years ago," she said in a thin, anxious voice. "When I born into the world... when my mother had died, and no one was willing to feed me, a woman who had lost her child, held me in her arms, fed me and loved me. Her face was a twisted mass of scar, she couldn't hear others' voice well, and the people went to another direction when they saw her, but I learned to love from her, and I loved her..." The big wet tears filled her eyes. She raised her head, stared at the old woman's face. "Forgive me! Your Jamaspa was killed to save my life."

Mithra's sobbing mingled with the old woman crying. The woman stroked the Mithra's head as she buried her head in her hands. "Motherhood is a choice, to love someone else and put her happiness ahead of your own without a doubt," she said as tears ran down her wrinkled face. "Jamaspa has done the duty of any good mother." Her lower lip quivered as words slowly made their way out of her mouth. "She'll be able to rest in peace now."

*****

The heavy wooden door was shut behind them with a loud sound. Now they were in the labor camp.

Astyages stared at the door before the men's moving shoved him roughly toward a long wide corridor. The Mannaean men stumbled along side-by-side, stunned and confused. At the end of the hallway, a group of black young men was pouring a bucket of water over each of them as they were entering the camp. The guards opened the ropes of their hand and foot, instead, put the heavy iron shackles on them and finally gave them a piece of millet bread.

Nobody said anything, exhaustion, humiliations, injustice, sickness, and the death of loved ones had broken their spirit and now they were only bodies that knew they have to move.

Astyages took the bread and quickly gained a bite of it. It was tasteless, but he was hungry enough to take it very well. He made himself chew and swallow. He glanced across the camp. The camp was well sited atop a low stony ridge that ran from north to south, a wide area, great location on the riverside for the building of the king's new palace. The massive palace was glaring on a gigantic hill in the middle of the camp although the building was not yet complete; it was easy to find that this unique building will be the most beautiful palaces in the surrounding land.

There was midday, the time of the slaves' short rest and lunch. The courtyard seemed almost empty at first sight, the sun was shining in the middle of the sky, and its hot rays were beating on salves brutally, and shadows were so welcome, a chance to dwell in diffuse rays, to rest and they had taken refuge in the shade of tall green trees. The chains rattled softly as Astyages stepped forward. He looked at the men, these squatting figures kept swallowing millet bread with a colorless stew. Some of the muscular men looked at Astyages with dull incurious eyes.

Astyages' eyes were looking for a place to sit, but suddenly a thin man ran out from behind him, gave him a hefty shove then bent down quickly and picked up a piece of bread from a young man's plate who was sitting on the ground. There was no reaction. The men were sitting in silence and eating their food. Astyages looked at the young man. He was in his late twenties, but he seemed like children. His narrow eyes followed the man as his thick tongue was seen in his half-open mouth. Astyages bent and put half of his bread in the young man's hands. The young man looked at him with his kind eyes and smiled.

"A fresh young newcomer;" a man said, sitting a little further, and grinning through his beard. "Soon you will feel the same!"

The man had tied a cloth around his head; he stared at Astyages with his tiny black eyes. He had described Astyages young, but he was not too much older. He was sitting in the shadow of the wall, stretching his long and toned legs and his empty dish was in front of him. The man scratched at his beard. "Come, you must learn to stay away from sunlight; otherwise you can't survive so much."

The man gathered his feet to open a place for Astyages as he went to one knee beside him. The young man immediately stood up, picked up his food dish and rushed to them. Astyages looked at his foot and realized he did not have the shackles and chain like the rest.

"You see? He's not one of us," the man said. "They feed him enough at least!"

"This is not a good excuse to steal his bread," Astyages said with a sullen face.

The young man sat beside him, his arms and legs were dappled by sunlight and the shadows of leaves. He gave out with a childish chuckle, and Astyages smiled. The tall man stared carefully at Astyages.

"You look like one of the Mannaean men," the tall man said. "What was your job in your land?"

Astyages paused for a moment. "I was a farmer," he said.

"A farmer!" The tall man said thoughtfully. "I'm from Babylon, but I know your language well. This place is full of Mannaean captives, although, we all are one nation now, the slaves' nation!" He pointed with his bony finger to the others. "Look at them. They all look alike, the hot sunrays have burned their skin, the hard work has made them scrawny, and hunger has made them harsh and hostile. It does not matter where we're from, we hate each other, and we are afraid of each other. I don't know why, but we are struggling just to survive."

"Maybe because you hope to escape from the camp someday," Astyages replied.

The man stared at Astyages, carefully. "Escape? They have forgotten thinking about it. You know, they say that no one dies here because they are already dead," the man said.

Astyages looked around thoughtfully. "There should be a way to escape, and I'll find it finally," he said.

"Do not rush young man and remember, don't speak with anyone about the escape, here, people spy on each other for a piece of bread," the man said with a sour grin.

The young man tore apart the loaf of bread, soaked in his fish stew and gave it to Astyages. "I know how to escape," the young man said with a thick, slobbery voice as if his tongue was too big for his mouth.

Astyages took the bread from him and made himself to smile. "How?" He asked.

The young man laughed like a child. "From the magic door!" He said.

Astyages just laughed in his face.

CHAPTER FOUR

LOST LOVES

Nineveh, 627 BC, Autumn

Hara entered without knocking. Mithra had leaned against the windowsill, looking up from the arched window at the sky, high above them a crow circled.

Hara stopped at the doorway, trembling, afraid to move as if she had gone back in time. *Eighteen years ago,* she thought.

*****

Lakaran, Assyrian forte, 646 BC, Autumn

Amitira had leaned against the windowsill. Her thick curly warm red-brown hair spilled over her shoulders, and her beautiful, unique honey golden eyes were staring into the darkness of the night, lost in thoughts.

Hara sat in bed with a weary and yellow face. She glanced at Amitira, but a sudden racking cough bent her over. Her maid moved to help her, but she waved her off, and after a moment, she recovered. They had stayed in a fortress in a border town for more than three months since Hara became ill mysteriously after her mother died. She was coughing, suffering from cold sweats and becoming thinner every day. The court's priests had said she should stay in a dry climate for a while, Nineveh's extremely humid weather made her worse. This was good news for the king because it meant she became out of sight... out of mind, so her brother had sent her to the mountains, on the border between Assyria and Mannea.

Unlike Hara, Amitira was full of life. They were the same age, but Amitira seemed taller and fitter than Hara. Amitira had lost her mother recently too, but unlike Hara, who had come to this isolated castle eagerly, Amitira had forced to leave the capital city. Yaafa had sent Amitira to the castle as Hara's friend and companion, an excuse to get rid of her beautiful and stubborn young sister who was a pain in her ass. Yaafa was a beautiful woman but not as much as her sister was. Amitira quickly stole the spotlight with her stunning and unique beauty. Her large liquid golden eyes held such boldness and intelligence that it was impossible for men not to be trapped by them. Her cheekbones were high, and her nose was perfect. Her long warm red hair was long and fluid, lying gently over her shoulder bones, kissing her soft skin. She was famous at the court as the second Semiramis. Not many men could stand against her beauty, let alone Yaafa' husband, the king Ashur Banipal who had sharp and greedy eyes for the beautiful women. Yaafa's son was now five years old, and Yaafa was using plenty of ways to keep herself looking younger, but she was nothing compared to Amitira.

The truth was, it was easier for Hara to be alone. Amitira's presence was unpleasant for Hara and even had added to her discomfort and illness. Hara was a spoiled child of a middle-aged mother who grew up in the king's palace, alone and isolated. Even in her youth, she had never been energetic, she was always so grumpy and so sensitive, and her mother's death and her illness had made her more sensitive and depressed. Everything made her upset sharply and sometimes she was crying for hours for no reason, on the other hand, Amitira was a strong, attractive, bright and also selfish and arrogant young girl. She did not like every bit of Hara's, and her coughing and tears just made her bored and angry.

It was almost midnight before Hara could rid herself of Amitira who did not even mind accompanying her and stared into the darkness amongst the garden trees through the window.

Hara took her eyes from Amitira, pressed her cheek to the cold, silk pillows. She preferred to think about something else, something more pleasant that she was enjoying thinking about it. A young medic man who the commander's wife had brought him to visit Hara, a Mannaean handsome guy who had a reputation for expertise in medicine. The commander's wife said he is the only one that would give Hara's health to her. The young man was coming every day to visit Hara. He was rubbing a poultice on her neck, pouring a bitter medicine in her mouth and spoke kindly to her for hours.

After only two weeks of treatment, Hara felt better. She was not coughing as much as before, slept easier through the night, and she was strong enough to sit on her bed, waiting for him. Gradually, Hara was waiting for Armaz every day with excitement. Hara was speaking about her life, her problems, and her secret feelings.

Hara was a quiet girl. She grew up in the royal family, so she had taught from childhood; every word that came out of her mouth could be an enemy who has the power to destroy her. It was the first time that she could trust someone... a man! However, Armaz was a genius, an extraordinary man, who talked about everything in an astonishing fashion, a handsome man with beautiful lips, magnificent teeth.

He never left her mind; he was always there. Her feeling was just indescribable. Hara was feeling Armaz was becoming her confidante, her anchor in a stormy ocean filled with chaos and sadness waves, someone who she desperately needed in her life.

I'm in love with him, Hara thought fearfully.

She resisted for a while. This feeling was so strange, unfamiliar and intimidating, but it stretched throughout her whole body, overwhelming, but made her feel happy. She was feeling it as a dangerous fire, but completely safe and pleasant at the same time. Now, Armaz was not a stranger, he knew Hara's mother had not come out of her room for two years and then she committed suicide by poison. He knew about the nights that Hara had to stay with her mother, listening fearfully to her speech with ghosts that she thought she saw them in the room. He knew Hara's brother, Ashurbanipal, the king of Assyria, did not allow anyone to marry with Hara because he was afraid of having a nephew who will claim his throne one day. Armaz was listening patiently to her words, and he tried to calm her.

Hara kept falling in love with him and waiting for his coming, each time was harder than the last. Every time her feeling got deeper. Every moment that Armaz was not beside her, she felt like the world stopped. Every time he was rubbing the ointment on her chest to ease the cough, it felt like he was untying all of her retroactive knots. For her, this was what falling in love was like, living a dream that she never wanted to end, a dream that she cannot bear to woke up and realize that ended.

A loud sound made her startle. Amitira had gotten up suddenly, and a goblet had fallen on the floor beside his feet. Her eyes shone, and she had a charming smile on her full lips. When she saw Hara's surprised look, she paused a little.

"I thought I'd better go to sleep," Amitira said. She had a warm smile on her lips as she left the room.

Hara preferred to be alone, but she was curious about Amitira's strange behavior. Amitira left the room quickly as Hara's eyes escorted her thoughtfully. She did not like to think about her now, preferred to remember the moments when Armaz rubbed the cold oil on her skin with his warm hands but she was curious by nature, and a mysterious force was dragging her thoughts to Amitira. Hara was suddenly conscious of how Amitira has had better behavior recently. Hara who had no care in the world but Armaz did not realize that Amitira was not complaining. She did not talk anymore about this fact that she was forced to live in an isolated place, far away from the Nineveh's luxury life, the feasts in the royal house and her magnificent palace just because of Hara. Even, she spent her evenings with Hara, although they could not find something to say, Hara was often lost in her thoughts and Amitira sat for hours, in silence.

"It's time for cough syrup, my Lady." Her maid entered the room, as Hara was thinking about Amitira's inexplicable smile.

The young girl helped Hara to sit on the bed and poured one spoon of a bitter syrup into her mouth. The taste of medicine in her mouth gave her discomfort, its flavor seemed unbearable, but it has prepared by Armaz, so she drank it with pleasure.

"How does Lady Amitira go to sleep early but wake up late?" Hara asked her maid.

The girl was her maid, but she had a heart-to-heart friendship with Amitira.

"I don't know… she's only sleeping," she said, and she left the room immediately.

Her stammering only deepened her suspicions. *There is a fire behind the smoke,* Hara thought. She was sure of it, but the medicine did not allow her to think more about it and her heavy eyelids closed.

*****

Hara coughed nervously. "Yet you don't even have abilities to find a proper dress?" She said as she threw a pink dress in her maid's face.

It was almost noon, just before Armaz come for a visit and Hara grew more and more nervous. The maid stripped her, then dressed her in a golden sheen. Hara took the silver mirror in her hand and looked at it carefully; she wanted to make sure she dressed appropriately. Her golden dress was pretty, but it showed the dark circles around her eyes more than before. This was the fourth time that she was mad at her maid for what she had worn since morning. Her white dress showed her face pale, and the black one showed her too thin. Hara smashed the mirror in her rage.

"Armaz will be here soon, and you haven't done shit yet," Hara shouted angrily. "Find me a fucking dress! A damn good one, otherwise I would say that the soldiers beat you in the garden so that you can't walk for a month."

The girl served Hara as her maid of honor from childhood, and she knew her madly anger. She was sure Hara was serious in what she said. She ran headlong into the closet room. She pulled out a blue dress, but she remembered that Hara had worn it a few days ago at her meeting with the medic man and she never wore it again.

The maid smiled unconsciously; she knew well why Hara took her time choosing a dress, she was in love. Whenever the medic man was at her side, she did not seem sick, she was kinder and gentler, and her pale cheeks flushed to red. The maid put aside the blue dress and picked up the purple one. Hara was waiting, upset and angry. She entered the room.

"Here you are, my Lady. This dress suits on your body. You didn't wear it for a long time, and purple is a perfect color to your face," she said in a sweet voice to please her lady.

She went to remove her dress, so afraid that she could not manage all the buttons. The maid took a hasty step backward, looking at her in her timid hope and her heart sank. Hara had grown so thin, and her oversized dress gown had hung loosely about her shoulders. The maid before Hara had a chance to see herself on the mirror, arrange her messy hair with tragacanth sap and gave some rings of her curly hair on her face. Then she slowly pulled the dress from the back to look better and helped Hara to sit straight up on the bed then she gave the mirror to her.

Hara looked quite pleased with herself. Her curly arranged hair that framed her face had reduced her thinness and showed her beautiful. Hara put down the mirror, smiled for the first time, almost warmly, and the maid sighed silently with relief.

There came a soft knock on her door.

"Come," Hara said; felt her heart collapsed in her chest. She knew this sound well. Armaz stopped at the doorway, elegant, handsome and happy as always.

Armaz smiled. "You are more beautiful today which shows you are much better!" He said.

Hara heard her heart beating in her ears, fast and pleasant. She dared to hope that Armaz loved her. If he did not love her, he could not be so kind. If he did not, he could not speak so sweet and lovely.

"I'm better today," Hara replied, trying to hide her voice trembling.

Armaz came forward and sat beside her bed. He managed a sweet smile on his face.

"But I know you are tired of staying in bed," he said.

"Yes," Hara replied and then hastily added, "Will you rub ointment on my chest today?"

Armaz laughed. "No, you must forget the bed and poultice. I'm a medic. I know well it's not the disease that has kept you in this bed. Your cough is sounding better, and you don't have a fever anymore. These signs show that your disease is gone, but you don't leave your bed because you're scared," he said.

"I'm not a coward." Armaz's insolence angered Hara's royal subconscious.

Armaz took Hara's hand. "You are afraid of returning to the palace, of enduring the difficulties that you had in Nineveh so you'd rather stay sick," he said with a smile as he stared into her eyes. "You have lost your courage for living. You need to find a strong incentive to live; something that gives you a sense of power, something that you can get up and fight for it," he continued.

Hara closed her eyes; she did not dare to look at Armaz's black eyes. "Something like love!" She mumbled.

Armaz put his head back and laughed loudly.

"Yes. Love and hate are the greatest motives for our behavior, and of course, love is better to drive your life," he said as he touched her forehead and immediately proclaimed. "No fever ... I thought you have told me all your secrets, but you still have untold secrets! Love, huh?"

Hara did not respond, but her smile and flushed cheeks confirmed Armaz's guess.

"I'll find your little secret, but now we have a more important job. You have to get up from the bed," Armaz said.

Hara stared at Armaz with wonder. "I can't," she said.

Armaz got up to help. "You can put your hand around my neck," he said. "This is the moment!"

He put his hand behind Hara; she stood hesitantly. "Trust me! You must get out of bed. You better hurry; you'll miss what I want to show you," Armaz said. "Do you know how beautiful the garden is in the fall?"

Hara put an arm around his waist, and Armaz pulled her frail body along easily. They went together to the extensive terrace. Hara wished this short distance, from the bed to the porch, became long enough for her to stay in his arms for hours, feeling the heat of his body against her. She closed her eyes, but they reached the terrace very soon, too soon for Hara. Armaz kept her with one hand while he was opening the door with his other hand.

"Now you can see the fall into the mountain; it's magnificent," Armaz looked at her and smiled. "Breath Hara; the mountain's subtle air is more efficient of any medicine," he said.

It was the magic hour when the sun dyed everything in gold, it stopped raining, and the clouds partially disappeared, allowing some sunrays to reach the garden. The cold autumn breeze after the rain welcomed her, like an old friend. The leaves were dancing from branch to ground, each a colorful flag. She felt the breeze, rich with the aroma of the earth, she could see how the trees were clad in the many hues of the soil, there was a calmness what she could feel, for the first time, feeling safe as if she has found an anchor during a storm. She closed her eyes and smiled.

"I knew that I could see this beautiful smile on your face," Armaz said.

Hara looked at his pretty face. There was nothing disproportionate in his face, but his beautiful face did not fascinate her. Armaz was the epitome of comfort for her. Hara never in her life had such support, she never able to achieve this sense of security. Hara needed this support to reach happiness and live without fear. She knew she should tell him about her feels.

"I must speak with you," Hara said to Armaz, who was looking at her with a lovely smile.

Armaz nodded. "Well, I listen to you."

Hara hesitated, then gathered up her courage and opened her mouth to speak but at that moment, a voice from the doorway drew their attention.

"Oh, you are here? I didn't expect Hara to be outside the room."

Amitira entered the porch, and Armaz stood up immediately. "Oh, good, you're here," he said.

Amitira sat next to Hara, on Armaz's seat and put a bunch of wildflowers on Hara's skirt. "I arranged them for you, the last mountain's flowers," she said with a sweet voice.

Hara put the bouquet aside of her skirt in disgust. "Do you know each other?" She asked.

"Of course, it's impossible to ignore a girl like her, she shines like a jewel," Armaz said excitedly.

Amitira looked at Armaz with a beautiful smile. He sat opposite her, the better position to see her, totally lost in watching her. Hara looked at them with a frown. Amitira in her purple dress seemed really like a great stone of ruby. The color suited of her bronze skin and had given to her honey golden eyes a wild beauty. Her beautiful body showed the dress more glamorous. Hara irresistibly touched her chest, where her dress had hung limply on her small breast.

Armaz and Amitira seemed to have forgotten her presence, and soon they were deep in talk lovingly. Hara did not hear anything, she just stared at Armaz, seeing Armaz's real smile. She had realized his usual smile was a kind medic's smile to seal the patient-physician relationship. Hara was trembling, she was extremely angry with herself; no doubt, she had mistaken his pity for love! *Hara, the daughter of the king of Assyria, allowed her mind to be captured by the illusions and take her to the border of mania,* she thought, *how could I forget a rival like Amitira?* Her poor little heart reproached itself for even that passing forgetfulness of its feeling.

A few moments of feverish enjoyment were followed by acute suffering. Hara did not stop looking at them, but they were too much absorbed in their mutual joy to notice her. The mountain's unsettled weather turned to another face. The sun had vanished behind a bank of low clouds, the cool breeze was replaced by a cold wind that made her shiver, and she felt the first drop of freezing rain hit on her face. Armaz and Amitira did not pay too much attention until the rain fell slashing down in a hard, cold torrent.

Armaz jumped up and rushed to Hara. "Oh, let me take you to bed, this cold wind is not good for you," he said.

Hara raised her hand to stop Armaz come closer. "That's not necessary, I can walk," she said, and stood, shaking,

"It is great; the mountain weather has made a miracle," Armaz said, surprised at the sudden rage in her eyes.

Hara managed a smile on her face. "I think I've found a motivation to get out of the bed," she shuffled closer with small stutter steps. When she saw Amitira, smiling her wicked smile, halted. Amitira was in purple silk; her appearance was greatly in her favor. She had all the best part of beauty, a pretty face, a perfect figure, and very pleasing dress. Hara's breath caught in her throat. Armaz rushed to her and Amitira offered her hand to help her to walk. Hara waved a hand, dismissing Armaz concern. "It is a chill, no more," she gave Amitira a sidelong glance. "Gods, I was a fool to think you don't know each other, you're absolutely right Armaz, my friend is too beautiful. And kind besides." Amitira drew her arm back, baffled.

Armaz gave her a bright smile. "I spoke only a simple truth that any man with eyes could see."

Hara did not take her eyes off her until she passed. "True, it's not only your opinion, but all men also say it," she said.

Her legs felt like pudding beneath her, and the coughing racked her so badly, but she did not allow they came to help her and finally threw herself on the bed, exhausted, the recently days reeling tipsily through her mind. Armaz picked up the jar of ointment from the table to rub it on Hara's chest. Hara could see jealousy in the icy glitter of Amitira's eyes for just one moment and the rage that she tried so hard to hide. She took the jar with a kind smile. "I can do this," she said as she sat on the bed, beside Hara.

Armaz looked at her the way all women want to be looked at by a man. "What kind of friend are you?" He said. "You are so kind and sweet!"

Armaz looked at Hara's cold face; her eyes were staring at the ceiling.

"I have to go, but I will come back to see you tomorrow," Armaz said. He went to the door but before he leaves, returned. "You wanted to tell me something, what it was?" He said to Hara.

"Nothing, it does not matter," Hara said without looking at him.

Armaz slightly paused and said. "Well, tomorrow we talk together."

Hara nodded, and Armaz went out.

Amitira opened the jar and frowned, she stared down at it as if the smell of it was about to make her sick. The pot was in Amitira's hand, but it was obvious that she had no interest to do this job.

"What kind of friend are you?" Hara made a sound that was half a laugh and half a roar of rage. "The kindness is not a habit with you, something you do not understand."

Amitira stared at her gloomily, put the jar on the table and took the ointment, shook it hastily. Hara's maid came into the room almost immediately. Amitira stood up.

"Come and rub this ointment on your lady's chest!" Amitira said to her.

"Come to me tonight, I don't like to be alone," Hara said before Amitira can leave the room.

Amitira stopped at the doorway, paused and said. "I want to go to bed early tonight."

Hara was still looking at the ceiling. "I wait for you tonight!" She said.

"I'm not your maid, you can't order me," Amitira said defensively.

"Then I'll have to say Armaz what you don't want him to hear," Hara said, with an archly smile. "I mean, you don't want to give him the wrong idea, do you?!"

"Okay, I'll come," Amitira agreed reluctantly. "I don't know what the fuck you want with me, but I'll come." She said dryly and went out.

Hara grabbed the mirror on the table, looked at herself, her curly hair that had framed her face, and her purple dress suddenly showed her very silly and ridiculous, like a court jester.

The maid was beside her, ready to rub the oil on her chest.

"You knew that, Huh?" Hara said, staring at her, through her clenched teeth. "You knew they love each other."

The maid swallowed, and opened her mouth ready to say something; Hara glanced at her angrily, grabbed her hair, and smashed her face on the table. An ear-splitting scream echoed through the castle and into the hall.

*****

Amitira went to the window to stare out into the night as she showed that she was not in the mood to have Hara's glancing suspiciously at her. Hara's maid sat in the corner of the room, sewing a new dress for Hara as was seen terrible bruises on her face. No one had anything to say, nor a desire for dialogue. All Amitira's senses were centered into the garden and Hara although sometimes looked at Amitira's face with disgust, was lost in her thoughts with a stern face.

Hara looked at Amitira again. She could not deny her stunning beauty, but on the other hand, Armaz was not the breed of man who only felt the need for a woman in bed. Something had been nagging at the back of his mind all day. *We have equal power to win him;* Hara thought as she stared at her beautiful, insolent, and hard face, *I'm powerful, as much as you are pretty*. An owl's voice was heard from the garden and Amitira who was sitting on the chair quickly stood up. The shine in her eyes and her flushed cheeks revealed everything.

"Sit down! I told you, you have to stay in my room tonight," Hara said violently.

"And I told you, I'm not your maid, you can't order me," Amitira said as she was going to the door.

"Don't go out, or else…," Hara shouted.

"Or else what? What are you doing? You want to beat me like your poor maid?" Amitira said as she stepped towards Hara with anger. "Yes, you have guessed right. I'm going to see Armaz, and you cannot stop me. I know you love him but don't bother yourself, Armaz loves me!"

Hara was staring at her. "Oh, Angels don't get angry with ease sweet girl!" Hara said with a mockery tone.

"I've tried to be kind to you all because Armaz asked me to do," Amitira said. "But you know what, he doesn't know you well; otherwise, he knew that you don't deserve kindness and love."

Hara felt the flames of never-ending rage burning in her heart. "He never gets a chance to know the real you as well. I'm sure he's dying to know what kind of business you did in Nineveh; the things that made your sister forced you to come to this isolated place. If he knew, he doesn't wait for you in that cold night in the garden," she said.

Amitira looked at the satisfied smile on Hara's red and feverish face. She was pale, and her lips were trembling. "You know your brother better than all people, and you know that I have no fault," she said, her voice was melted by rage.

Hara laughed. "I'll talk to him, wench," she said. "Then let him decide if he wants to be with you."

"We're in love, and we don't have secrets," Amitira said proudly.

Hara scowled again, her face glowering suspicion. "You're lying."

Amitira grinned. "I have nothing to fear!" She said as she put her hand to the doorknob.

"When I offer him to be the official court physician, he will soon forget you." A fit of coughing seized Hara as she tried to continue. She clutched the rail for support and spat over the side. "For men, power is more important than love," she wheezed. "He will be missed you, at first months perhaps, but in a month he will forget even your name, and be happy!" Hara said what she had thought about it for all day.

Amitira blasted in a burst of laughter. "How can you expect Armaz love you while you don't know him at all? You want to buy him by a position at the court of Assyria?" She said between her laughs. "The poor girl! Know that he hates of your brother and all the courts of Assyria, for him your brother is not the great king of Assyria, he is a brutal animal that has massacred many of his land's people. Never spoke about your offer because you make him very annoyed."

The owl's voice was heard again from the garden. Amitira opened the door, but she turned to Hara at the last moment. "Armaz isn't yours, forget him!" She said. "I'm not asking you to do it for me; I'm asking you to do it for yourself."

Hara heard the door shouting loud sound. She closed her eyes; she was feeling a fierce heat inside. She felt suddenly a fire flared in her heart and devoured her in its flames. She got up from the bed. She was burning in fever, but she did not feel weakness.

Her maid looked at her, shocked. "Rest my Lady; exciting is not good for you... my Lady," she said, trembling.

Hara kicked savagely at her chest with a heel, the maid dragged herself back to protect herself of her attacks, but Hara was not looking for her, she went to the window and stared into the garden. It did not take very long before she saw Amitira, running into the yard and a little further Armaz came out from the shelter of a large tree. He stepped further and hugged her so hard that Hara thought her ribs might break. He leaned down and softly kissed her lips. Hara turned her face quickly, her knees were trembling, but she did not need to sleep on the bed. She was feeling a strange power in her body, a power that had kept her firmly on her trembling knees. Armaz's voice echoed in her ear, 'Love and hate are the greatest motives for our behavior.' Hara felt a burning in her heart, love would not be her motive, but she knew how to make hate as leverage to get up from the bed.

"Tell me, bitch, what else you know that I don't know about it?" Hara said to her maid.

*****

Hara had worn a black dress that showed her much thinner and gathered her hair behind her head tightly. Hara had not slept the night before, she was aching from head to foot with fatigue, but she could not sleep. Hara was sitting there in an armchair, looking out of the window at the pouring rain with a pale face and fixed wide-open eyes. The beautiful garden that had delighted her yesterday did not raise any of happiness in her, and she was looking at it with a sullen face. Her maid sat propped against the wall behind, but she had fallen asleep.

Armaz's steps sound was heard, first from the staircase then the hallway. Hara pricked her ears up and listened to Amitira's whispering mingled with her giggle. Their laughing was a stone bouncing across a glassy lake, creating ripples of mirth. She shuddered with aversion but then heard Amitira walking away down the corridor.

Hara made a sign with her hands that showed her maid should leave her alone and she obediently went to the back room.

"What? God! Hara, is it really you?" Armaz stepped closer and took her hand. "I can't believe you're in such health!" He said.

Hara looked at Armaz and smiled. "I feel better, much better!" She said.

"It's great but a little early for sitting beside an open window, isn't it?" Armaz said as he closed the window and the curtain, smiling. "So, tell me what's going on?"

Hara shrugged "Nothing, I just feel a strange power in my body."

"I don't know I should be happy or sad, but that means you don't need my help anymore. It seems I must go to my city...," Armaz said.

"Or maybe not, if I offer you to be the special physician of the Assyrian court, what would you say?" Hara said immediately.

"I am not a physician who is suitable for the royal pains... I enjoy being among people," Armaz replied immediately with a grin.

"Are you sure? Maybe you hate the Assyrians?" Hara said.

"If I hated the Assyrians, I was not in this castle?" Armaz said, smiling.

"But I heard you come here for a specific purpose, isn't it?" Hara said as she was staring at him. A ruse to convince the servants. This was what she had learned since she was a kid.

Armaz's smile faded and just for a moment, his eyes his brown eyes watched her warily then he extended his hand to touch her forehead. "I think you have a fever," he said, laughing.

Hara grabbed his hand. "Don't pretend like you don't know what I'm talking about," she said; her fingers left his hand, almost reluctantly. "You're a spy? Aren't you?" She had nothing to lose.

"I'm not spying for anyone!" Armaz said.

"You came here to identify where the breach is in this fortress for takeover," Hara said.

"No!" Armaz said dryly.

"Identify our source and soldiers...," Hara said, no attention to his word.

"I said no!" Armaz tried to manage a smile. "Enough, I came here to heal you," he said and extend his hand to ointment jar.

Hara glanced at Amitira through the window; she sat on a stone bench. *Waiting for Armaz for sure,* Hara thought. "I know my brother, the king of Assyria, he doesn't have mercy. You're not the only one who is in danger."

Armaz followed her look direction and saw Amitira in the garden; he drew his hand back unconsciously.

"Trust me; I can help you, Amitira and you!" Hara said. "Is it true that I said?"

Armaz's eyes were pinned on Amitira.

"Everybody knows about the relation between Amitira and you, she's from the royal family, if she gets caught, her life would be more painful than death," Hara said, staring at Armaz. "I ask you again, are you here to spy for the Median king?"

Armaz looked at her. "Do what you want with me but don't get her into trouble!"

"Proved, that's what I've been telling you," Hara said.

The Lord Commander of the castle, following by two soldiers came out of the closet room; he looked shocked. The soldiers rushed to Armaz and caught him.

Armaz was staring at Hara; he had stood there without any resistance. "Why?" he said.

"Because you need to learn…," a bad cough disturbed Hara's conversation; she drew in a deep breath and slowly released it. "A spy could not love a royal girl." The soldiers dragging Armaz out of the room. "The medic has an accomplice," Hara said before the commander had a chance to leave the room.

He turned to Hara sparingly.

"She is in the garden, arrest her now!" Hara added.

"You don't mean that … Lady Amitira?"

"You heard what I said!" Hara said dryly.

"But she is Lady Yaafa's sister… I can't…,!" the commander stammered in a low voice.

"And I am the sister of the king of Assyria," Hara shouted. "Seize her right now; you're looking like an accomplice in this."

"NO my Lady, I just think…"

Hara interrupted him. "If you had the ability to think you never let a spy come here, so you just follow my orders."

"Yes, my Lady," he said as he bent his knee, bowed his head, and withdrew.

Hara caught the movement in the mirror from the corner of her eye. Her maid stared at her, her eyes winded.

"Run, don't even look back because I promised to protect you from the soldiers, not myself," Hara said as she was looking at her maid in discuss.

The maid left the room, running. Hara peered outside at Amitira; she was sitting on a stone bench, waiting as she had a beautiful rose in her hand. The sound of loud footsteps caused her to turn back. Her soft voice changed as she was speaking with the soldiers and became harsh and commanding. Amitira shoved them back and made to run, but a soldier caught her arm before she'd gone a step. She shrieked and kicked as she was dragged into the garden, towards the old stables.

Hara closed the curtains, held each other, and the lights down low. She was not pleased, not sad even not satisfied. Hara began to cough, deep, throbbing, hacking coughs that shook her tiny body. She sat on the bed; she did not feel anything as if the soldiers brought her heart out of her room.

*****

Hara was lying on the couch in her room, staring at the ceiling above her head, like yesterday and the day before. A statue of Ishtar, the goddess of love, war, fertility, and sexuality, hanging from the white paint ceiling was looking at her, blaming. She closed her eyes, the goddess of love showed no mercy for her.

Through the garden, she heard men shouting, and once a horse whickered nearby. She sat on the bed, feeling chilled with the cold sweat, coughing frequently. Suddenly the door opened and a maid who was so excited that had forgotten nock the door came in. "My Lady, the great queen is here; can you believe it?" She said and left the room without waiting for her answer.

"I can!" Hara said through her clenched teeth.

She got up horribly, she should take care of her appearance, but she did not have a maid who helped her to manage her curly rebellious hair. She rushed to the closet room, but she even did not get the chance of entering. The commander's wife led Yaafa to Hara's room and stood, bowed her head respectfully. Yaafa was at the doorway; wrapped in heavy cloaks of thick grey wolf fur, beautiful, adorned as always.

Hara knew well how to behave in front of others, bent her knee, and bowed her head. Yaafa gave her most kind smile.

"Sweetheart, I'm so glad to see you all right." Yaafa stepped forward, took Hara's hands and let her stand. "Look at her," she said. "You know, you look more attractive than the previous." She turned to the commander's wife, smiling. "Please leave us alone, I haven't seen her for so long."

The door shut and Hara went to her bed. "How could you meet my messenger before my brother?" She said as she sat on the bed.

"How big a fool you are," Yaafa took off her cloak and threw it on the bed beside Hara, regardless of her leering. "Your messenger was my spy!"

"Spy?" Hara said, sharply.

"Yes," Yaafa said, she kept her voice low, but Hara could hear the fury in her tone. "Did you honestly think I've settled onto the cushions in Nineveh, unaware of what's happening here? Or I have forgotten my stupid sister?"

Hara glanced up at her in discuss. "If you had a spy why didn't you come here before your sister really messed everything up?"

"Everything was going fine, exactly what I needed. Amitira was in love with that stupid guy and she got the hell out of here sooner or later." Yaafa gave Hara a look filled with fury and anger. "It is you that messed it up!"

"He is a Median spy, you expect me to ignore the rules?" Hara said.

Yaafa gave her a sour grin. "You just say stupid stuff; start making better excuses than it." She leaned towards her. "Do you know what that could do to me in that damn court?" She laughed, a sort of sweet disgust. "Although, you only think about yourself."

"That's not an excuse," Hara said, irritated. "I got his confession; didn't your spy tell you that?"

"Stop explaining, I've had enough," Yaafa said. "I've been in the carriage, without rest, for much longer than two days. I needed a hot bath, a warm bed." She got up, ready to go. "This can't go any farther. It won't, my little sister in law. I'm putting an end to this, tonight."

"How?" Hara asked sharply.

Yaafa stared at her. "Easy, as I expected." Hara stared at Yaafa's eyes, as green as the rope of emeralds around her throat and watched the flames of wickedness into her eyes. "I let them run away, let them believe they're just too smart." She giggled like a little girl. "The king will hear Amitira ran away with a young guy, that's it, no more."

"You won't stop me," Hara's words broke in a harsh cough. "I know how much are you hiding from my brother? Into your bed … into your arms... remember that young man, your special guard," she said, her words broke up in a fit of coughing.

Yaafa was looking at her calmly. "Well, I have something to tell him too," she said.

"I have done nothing wrong what should I be afraid of?" Hara growled.

Yaafa smiled; a mocking smile. "Everybody knows you loved that Mannaean guy."

Hara felt the blood rushing to her face. She put her head down, hoping to hide her blushing.

"You were in your bedchamber for hours and who knows what you did." Yaafa waited a few seconds. "You know what is more important for the king of Assyria, his abounded queen adultery or his sister trying to get pregnant, for a son, who could be our king someday." then put a finger under Hara's chin and forced her to look up into her eyes. "You'll be buried, here, immediately, noiselessly." Yaafa's fingers gently tuck Hara's hair behind her ear. "You need me, whether you like it or not, so just do as I say!"

Hara heard wheezing from her chest, which was had not heard for a long time. She grabbed a little bottle from the night table and took a big sip of the bitter syrup. She remembered Armaz's memories as bitter as the medicine.

Hara stared at Yaafa. "Listen to me," she said. "I got a plan… I got a plan to fix it."

Yaafa frowned in disbelief. "What the hell are you thinking?"

"Listen," Hara said, trying to take a deep breath. "Amitira will run away with… with him, but to the depths of hell, because the arrows of the guards will catch them."

Yaafa shook her elegant head. "A wise man avoids edged tools;" she said. "We can do it quietly." She stood up, ready to leave.

"It's for the interest of us, not only for my own," Hara said, quickly.

"How?" Yaafa said.

"You know your sister well enough!" Hara stood in front of her, "shall we make a bet on how many days her love will last?" She stepped forward, stared into her eyes. "She will be back on her feet soon."

Yaafa arched an eyebrow. "I accept! But under one condition, let me handle it to the end," she said, in words that would brook no argument. "You won't even do your own dirty work!"

"I have one condition too," Hara said in a sudden rush. "I'll pick the archer, the damn best archer in this land."

Yaafa grinned. "What are you afraid of?" She said.

Hara shrugged. "I just know I can't trust you."

Yaafa let her eyes linger on Hara's face then went to the door. "Put a comb through your hair for God's sake. How did you hope to gain him with this mess?" She said with a mockery voice and left.

Her fury was a fire in her chest like a burning tie; Hara grabbed the wooden carved chair and smashed it on the floor.

*****

Yaafa entered the dark room; it was clean but too small. The only light was the dusty light coming from the small back window. It did not look like a prison, probably one of the guard's room. The soldier bowed his head, withdrew. Yaafa's eyes found hers. Amitira squatted on a bed of dry grass. She was wearing a gown, a dark yellow gown, but torn.

Amitira looked sad but when she saw her sister, sat straight up, smiled an arrogant smile. "I could almost smell you; they didn't do this without your involvement!"

"Well done, little sis!" Yaafa said in disgust, "but if you have a good nose, you can smell a dangerous mix of jealousy and madness, not my involvement. There's no point for me, imprisoning you for being a traitor … do you have any idea what I'll be through." She sat beside her sister, carefully; her bed looked so dirty. "This is the result of your stupid game with that devil girl."

Amitira turned her face, without any word, her head proudly erect; she stroked her hair back from her face. "This is not a game, I love him!"

Yaafa laughed derisively. "You're not capable of loving; if you loved him, you didn't this to him." She moved her face closer to hers. "Do you know what his punishment is? They peel him off, live as if he is onion or potato," she said with a grin.

Amitira swallowed. "You're lying, isn't it?"

"I wished you were as wise as you are beautiful," Yaafa said.

"She's lying, you know it," Amitira said hastily.

"Only two of you know who's lying here," Yaafa said dryly.

"Please save him, please!" Amitira said.

Yaafa looked at her; she had never seen her sister so sad and innocent. Amitira was a burning wheel, unreliable and arrogant, with the unconscious desire to destroy but she was looking so miserable now.

"Preserving of his life has no use to me," Yaafa said. "I'm here to rescue you."

"No, no without him," she whispered, one lone tear rolling down her cheek.

"I worked it out so you two can run away," Yaafa said with a sullen face.

Amitira took Yaafa's hands in a solid grasp. "Will you really do that for me?" She said, her eyes shone with joy.

Yaafa looked at Amitira's dirty hands with disgust and pull out of her grasp. "I'll do it for myself!" She said, cleaning her hands.

"I love you!"

Yaafa raised her head, shocked, looked at Amitira who was pouring tears. She was almost eighteen, and without her usual courtier make-up, she seemed quite a teenager, an innocent, gullible teenager. She stole her eyes from her sister almost immediately, remembered Hara's word. Amitira's beauty was stunning; a woman with an irresistible charm, no man can defy her will. Especially the king, her husband who was a swinger man.

She got up immediately to hide her nonplussed face.

"Stop crying like a little girl, get some rest, you need to be prepared for tonight!" Yaafa said as she was going to the door.

"Yaafa!"

Yaafa turned to her sister.

"Thank you, not only for today… I never thought you love me," Amitira said.

*****

The deepening purple twilight was gradually filling the cloudless sky. Yaafa took a deep breath eagerly, letting her feelings out. She went a few steps further up, then stopped again. "Where's the man?" She asked the master guard who was leading her toward the castle.

"The medic?" He asked with a sullen tone. "Underground the fort, in the dungeon, My Queen."

"Lead me there, I want to see him!" Yaafa said.

"That place is not proper for our Queen!" The master said.

Yaafa looked at him, a middle-aged man, handsome and very tall with a sullen face. Yaafa knew this kind of men very well. It mattered not where the queen went, but he believed the power should be kept within men.

Her full lips pressed together in anger. *How I hate the grown men with their seas of doubts and objections!* Yaafa thought, raised her voice. "Don't need anyone worrying about me and I damn sure don't want someone telling me where I can go... Lead on!"

The iron door opened with a thin sound like an animal screaming in pain. He was stood up against a wall, iron shackles held him hard against the cold stone wall. The sound of the door brought Armaz awake, and he realized somebody came. A deep wound was seen above his eyes and a dark bruise on his cheek but still looked handsome.

Yaafa moved up her hand to release the master who stood in front of the door with his sullen face. The door closed. Yaafa walked down, the rotted wooden steps descending into the darkness of the dungeon.

"Who are you?" Armaz asked.

"I've been a bit curious about you," Yaafa said as she stepped forward. "I've wondered what this man would be like, who was fool enough to love my monster sister."

Armaz smiled. "I should have guessed… you look so much like Amitira," he said.

The queen moved further, laughed and tossed her red-brown curls. "Love has blinded you young man; there is not even a likeness between her and me!" She said.

Armaz nodded slowly. "You're more like her than you know. You have very similar gestures and a sweet voice," he said.

"I suppose you don't know women well!" Yaafa said. "Those aren't similarities, but flirtatious!" she stared at his face with a grin.

"How can you say I'm wrong? Just you can talk so sweet and gentle, and yet so strange and wild," Armaz said. "My Lady, you're so similar to my love." His voice was hoarse with remembered her. "She has a hard time, I'm terribly sorry to make her suffer."

"Don't be, her place is very better than you," Yaafa said calmly.

Armaz moved slightly to ease the stabbing pain in his wrist. "You know well she is not a traitor, she loves Assyria, you must punish me not her."

Yaafa moved her hand impatiently. "Nobody likes to watch a stupid show twice; I already watch that in Amitira's room."

"But l am guilty!" Armaz insisted.

Yaafa looked at him thoughtfully. "I don't know who is guilty, but for me, it is easier to forgive you than her," she said.

"I understand how you feel my Queen! She has told me everything," Armaz said.

"Everything?" She repeated quite spontaneously. "You have heard that was advantageous for Amitira stupid boy!"

"She had told me more than I wanted to know and it was to her disadvantage," Armaz said. "You don't know her and it's not your fault, she is tough, uncommunicative and moody. She had a tough look, but in fact, she's a sensitive girl, who afraid of the unfairness of people. A cat that acts like a tiger!"

"What are you saying? A cat?" Yaafa laughed, angrily. "She is a serpent with golden eyes!" She stepped a little further. "But we have the same blood in our vein. I'm an eagle who knows how to walk over her..."

She screamed, a giant rat running rapidly past.

"Don't be afraid, your smell of perfume get it to run away, it would prefer me," Armaz said, smiling. "I told you; you have learned to pretend you're bold."

Her ear caught the sound of footsteps echoing along the path through a long corridor. She looked at Armaz. "You know what, we're not ordinary people, if we were, I am sure that we could be perfect friends."

"Life is not a good playmate, it was playing the game in its own way," Armaz said bitterly.

*****

Hara grabbed his wrist before he reached the gold coins. "Look, ensure your arrow goes exactly where I want it to. This is a very, very important thing to me."

Ebigil, the best archer in Assyria looked at her, fearfully. "Yes, your Highness."

"So soon enough, good things should happen to you," Hara said.

"Don't worry my Lady, it's easy as pie," Ebigil said as he was collecting the coins.

Hara looked at him sharply. "All right, leave!" She felt a bitter hatred for this man who wanted to follow her wish.

Ebigil glanced at her and left the room immediately.

"Are you satisfied now?" Yaafa said.

"I won't be satisfied till she's alive," Hara said dryly.

"The fever has cooked your wits. You should probably get some rest," Yaafa said as she went to the door.

"Where are you going?" Hara asked sharply.

Yaafa lifted her thin black eyebrow. "Surely you don't expect me to sit here and watch your deadpan face? I'm going to get some rest," she said. "The commander's wife throws a banquet in my honor tonight; I don't want to look tired and ugly."

"How can you be so cold-blooded?!" Hara was staring at her in disgust.

"And how could you be so wicked like this?" Yaafa said with a mocking smile.

"Making love with those young and sweet seventeen years old boys seems like such a miracle to you," Hara said from behind. "You're no longer the angry, depressed woman that I knew."

Yaafa hesitated for a few moments, wiped anger from her face and turned to Hara, smiling. "Oh yes, try it," she said. "It will be much better than a one-sided love which dies on its own." Yaafa opened the door, a special young guard, hardly seventeen had stood in front of the door. "If you want I'll send my maid to make you like a real royal girl, Huh?"

Hara looked at her with full of hatred. "I'm not really familiar with that kind of parties, I'll stay here in my room, go alone."

Yaafa shrugged. "Your life depends on you, young girl!" She said before leaving the room.

*****

Waiting, it was the only thing that Hara could do, on her bed, with open eyes, staring at the ceiling in her dark room, while she fell prey to uncontrollable but quiet fits of coughing sometimes.

Hara turned her head slowly, listening to music. The castle blazed lights from every room, and she could hear the music from the vast hall, where a woman was singing a silly song about love. *Is there someone who believes this song?* Hara thought. She could hear Yaafa's booming laughers, echoing across the castle. She could imagine her, beautiful and natty, seized by the young commanders that tried to flatter her.

"It's true, men really do love bitches!" Hara said through her clenched teeth. She coughed, took a swallow of medicine, its bitter taste gave her a clumsy squeeze that reminded Armaz. She smashed the bottle on the wall and coughed again more violently, following by gasping for air. It seems there was no air in the room. She rushed barefoot across the marble floor out onto the terrace, sighed deeply to get enough air. A thunder rolled, seemed to crack the air, and rain hammered down. She leaned against terrace pillar, stood, gazing down upon the garden. The music was heard louder here, but Hara paid no attention to the women and men, she stared at the end of the darkness ahead, on the south end of the garden. A dungeon had swallowed Armaz. Her face twisted in terrible anger, her dark eyes shining sadly through the dark, she balled her hands into fists.

"Damn it, damn it, damn it," Hara shouted as she sobbed hysterically. "My damn heart, why don't you stop thinking about him? Why are you still worried about what happens to him? It is time to let it go." The rain and tears mingled on her face, salty tracks blending into the fresh sky-fallen trickles. "He doesn't deserve your love, can't you see that? You trusted him, and he betrayed you." She slipped on the rain-slick pillar slowly and crashed onto her knees, cursing. "Stop it, you little fool, stop it," her words caught in her throat. Her cough became a terrible thin whistle as she strained to suck in air. "He deserves such a fate!" She forced herself to say.

She heard the distant brazen blare of horns, the thin skirling of pipes faint beneath the sound of the rain beating on the wet ground. Hara startled by the sound of the horns although she already knew why those men had made noises. "Nearly there!" She whispered in terror.

Hara rushed toward the door. The music had died, and the guest hall was in a constant uproar of the guests. She got out by the back door. It was like one big party, almost everyone got drunk, and she hoped to reach there before others arrived. The night rain fell cold and hard, whipping on her face, lashed at her cheeks. Hara could not hear her own footfalls beneath the sound of the thunder. She was thoroughly wet and numb. The force of her every step caused shallow puddles to spit aggressively, her breath was coming in gasps, and the cold air was burning her injured lungs. She was not getting enough air, wracking coughs shook her entire body, her bare foot slipped on some wet mud, and she fell down. Her nostrils flaring at the scent of blood.

The horn blew again, two long blasts. Hara heard noises coming from the castle. She was tired, and her chest hurt, but she got up and plodded through the stony path. Nobody was in the watchtower; Yaafa had already prepared everything. Hara fell up the stairs; her ears started to hurt from the thumping going on in her chest. Her chest burned and she could hardly put one foot, but she kept moving. Nothing could stop her but faint.

She saw his face in profile, squatting beside the solid castle wall, nocked an arrow to his bowstring. He bent the bow into an arc, pulling the string tight around the other notch. Hara sucked in air and screamed. She ran with all her strength, and pushed him down to the ground, breathing hard, shaking. Ebigil dragged himself to the corner of the wall, stared at her in stunned disbelief.

Hara bent over the wall, she could see them, on a huge white horse, pounding past at a gallop.

In the yard, screams, running footsteps, the whinny of frightened horses, and the frantic barking of the castle dogs... tied up into one. Hara covered her face with both hands, and Ebigil heard her bitter sobbing mingled with the sound of a fit of coughing.

*****

Yaafa was fulfilled with the party. She did not worry about what was happening in the garden. Her beautiful eyes, dull with wine, met a young soldier's steady blue gaze. She smiled, lifted her goblet and began to drink her wine as she studied the young man. He was only an ordinary young man, dark brown-eyed hawk, piercing eyes, narrow nose with a vague hump, with hair the color of an autumn leaf. He could not be much over twenty, but she liked the young men, those who still have not mastered the basic skills of violent.

The young man slowly stepped toward her.

"What's going on in the garden?" Yaafa asked, trying to coquet with him.

"I don't know," the man said. "My Queen enchanted me with her beauty… all I see is her dark green eyes shone like twin emeralds in the grand dining hall…"

That was another quality that attracted her to the very young men; still, the romantic delicacy was not dead in them.

"He is waiting for you, My Queen!" Her maid whispered in her ear.

Yaafa smiled with an intellectual coquetry, glanced at the young man and then left.

Ebigil bent his knee when the queen entered. He was in a muddy set of the castle guard clothes.

"How did you?" Yaafa asked.

"As my Queen commended, they ran away."

"Well done," Yaafa said. "I'll order our men to bring your beautiful young wife to your house, immediately. Go."

Ebigil left the room respectfully.

"Find out what's going on and tell me what you see," Yaafa said to her maid.

The vast hall was at the end of a narrow corridor. She strolled, trying to hold her head high but she felt the earth rocking beneath her and her mind drifting in and out like the tide. She laughed. She knew that she had a little bit too much to drink, as always. She stumbled and leaned against the wall, suddenly someone grabbed her from behind, she wanted to scream, but the young man's firm and full lips pressed on her lips and made her silent.

*****

Ancient Land of Mannaeans, 627 BC, Autumn

"Translate what I'll say to her, word by word," Hara said to Savrina as she went toward Mithra. "Don't believe you are here because you have a kind aunt who is happy about finding her lost niece." She stood in front of Mithra, grinned. "You are here because your face, your face is an asset that holds its value well. So you must be careful." She stared straight into Mithra's eyes, her body shook with disgust and a dry cough. "That asset earn nothing for us if you be a naughty girl."

The coughing broke her speech. When she could look at Mithra again, she was staring at her like Amitira, arrogant and bold.

"You'll go to the slave market again if you couldn't learn how to look at me."

Mithra was looking at her, without one change in her angry face.

"If you want to die, I can't stop you, but I have to say maybe it will be so much worse," Hara said as she took a deep breath. She straightened her back, lifted her chin a bit, and stuck out her chest. "There's no mercy in Yaafa's heart, for you or anyone you loved, for example, that handsome Mannaean man."

Mithra got up; Hara could see what she wanted in Mithra's eyes. She laughed. "Don't be afraid." She was feeling better, "I didn't say anything about him to your aunt, not yet," she said, smiling.

Mithra could feel the sweat drench her skin and the thumping of her heart against her chest. She forced herself to remain impassive, but Hara saw her fingers curled into a fist, nails digging into her palm and heard her rapid breathing.

"I know what kind of slant-eyed savage you are, the living descendants of Semiramis but I'm a royal family member, too, the daughter of the great king of Ashur. I'm not merciless, at least not as much as you." she weighed Mithra long and carefully with her eyes. "He's in labor camp. You won't have to worry about him… yet!"

Hara went to the door with firm steps. "Learn our language to her, as soon as possible," she said to Savrina before leaving the room.

Mithra's heart was pounding harder as if horses were galloping in her chest. Nothing in her face betrayed her fear; it was a mask of defiance, what she used to be. "What the hell do they want from me?"

Savrina knew how the fear looked like for Mithra. She was determined to find a way, not desperate. She came to her. "Didn't you hear what she was saying? They need you, you have all the power in your hands." She cupped Mithra's face, and forced her to look at her. "You have gotten the power from them. Be armed with wisdom power, not your physical power," she said then buried her face in her chest to let proud Mithra hid her tears.

*****

The great king, Ashur, had the will to make his home on the river floor, a palace of coral and gems but the sandy soils of the river, potentially undermining the structure, so the slaves had to work tirelessly to do the king's will. After ten years, they had made an enormous mountain, of the rough, black stones. The king has passed away, but the palace was built for the next king on that huge handmade mountain.

The white limestone was as large as a carriage was used for building the palace of coral. The stones were tied onto sleds and pulled up on wooden tracks, which were anchored on the palace building.

Astyages and a tall, slender black guy sat down on the ground, panting. The soldiers let them rest until the next loads got there. His skin was now polished copper, and a thick beard had covered her thin face. He got calluses on his hand and was seen his bruises through his torn clothing. He threw a look around, unlike Mannea, there was no mountain, the earth was flat, under the burning sun. Looking up, he saw the sun shine brighter than he ever knew before. *Their sun is ruthless precisely like themselves,* Astyages thought as he wiped sweat from his forehead with the back of his arm.

He looked down the line of men without an exact purpose, but something had caught his eye. A little distance away, at the end of the line, a middle age man's eyes rolled backward, and his body went limp, he took a gasp of air and a faint. Everything was just happening so fast. The heavy block of limestone which they were dragged, fell down the hillside. Two men ran away, but a thin young black man, the first person on the line, had no chance to flee. The sand pinned his arms to his body as he struggled to release the heavy rock on his foot that was dragging him down.

At the last moment, Astyages grabbed the rope still dangling there. He held on the string, his feet slipped on the stony ground but met no resistance. Finally, Astyages hooked his hands on a stone hole and drew back a few steps hardly.

"Why are you looking at me like ghosts? Help me!" Astyages shouted.

No man came forward; they were looking at him with their nonsense eyes. The ground escaped beneath Astyages' foot and dragged him forward. He caught at the hole deeper with desperate hands. From under his nails, blood splashed on the stone, his knees rubbed against the stone and cried under the weight of the man's body. He took a deep breath, twisted the rope around his arm, cried in pain and anger, and pulled the rope, dragged the man over almost to the edge of the cliff. The men were getting excited, and the man struggled to come up but a dreadful hit of a sword cut the rope.

Astyages fell on his back and heard the man's terrible scream following by the sound of the disintegrated block and his body at the same time.

He looked up; the commander of the camp had stood in front of him. "Whoever you are and whatever your past may be, remember this: you are SLAVES now!" He shouted in their face. "Slaves could not be a fuckin hero, slaves do not make decisions, and it is not for slaves to want." The men around exchanged uneasy looks. The commander's face was expressionless with no sign of feelings. His dark hollow eyes showed that he had not emotions. "Slaves work, hard work to survive." He stepped to Astyages, sheathing his sword, glanced at him contemptuously. "You better watch yourself... slave!"

"You know him?" A tall strong man who had stood beside Bertkaameh whispered in his ear.

"A farmer... well, that's what he said," Bertkaameh said. "But I think he is from a Median royal family!"

"How'd you know he was one of them?" The man asked.

"I saw him on his first day, didn't look at all like a farmer, no callus, no sunburn, and he was polished, very quiet in his manner, deferential, observant..." Bertkaameh said as he stroked his long beard as usual. "I no doubt my guess."

"Maybe this guy can find a stone to put in that thing," the man said.

Bertkaameh nodded, said nothing.

*****

The night sky freckled with stars. The camp always looked different at night. Everything had looked even differently as if the daytime stones had gone to bed and sent more ominous versions of themselves to take their places slightly.

111

Astyages was lying motionless on the musty straw-stuffed mattress, next to a big rock. Hooraan was the only person near to him, as always. His narrow eyes were staring out into the darkness, his mouth half opened; no one could know what was going on in his six-year-old mind.

Bertkaameh sat beside him. "Astyages, are you asleep?"

"Hum," Astyages said without opening his eyes.

"You're not still mad at me, are you?" Bertkaameh said.

"I am seriously getting pissed off right now." He opened his eyes, stared at Bertkaameh. "You let him die, you and your friends."

"He wasn't our friend!" Bertkaameh said. "They're an invading tribe."

"Yeah?! But you said we had built a new nation after capture, slaves' nation."

"Do you really think we could be friends? It's ridiculous!" Bertkaameh growled. "Do you think we could be human here?" He moved his face closer. "We need to get out of here."

"Don't talk to anybody about escape and trust nobody! You said it once," Astyages said calmly and lay down again.

Bertkaameh took a deep breath impatiently. "Yeah, but now, I know you, you can't be a spy," he said.

"And why should I trust you?" Astyages said, with a sullen face.

"Stop being stubborn and listen," Bertkaameh lowered her voice until it was barely audible. "I have something in mind, a plan, but do you want to hear the end of this story or not?" He said sharply.

"Go ahead. I'm listening!" Astyages said indifference.

Bertkaameh cautiously peered around. "I know how to open the shackle," he said. "I have found something, two hammer hitting would be enough."

"That's all you got, huh?" Astyages said.

Bertkaameh was startled by his apathy. "It is not the one thing, after that, we only need a few minutes to get to the camp, behind the fortress the wall has been cracked, it'll help us to climb up easily." He looked at Astyages, excited. "With each full moon the river rising fast, we'll jump in the river, on the hill across the river, my friend knows a person who takes us to the border." He hesitated, then gathered up his courage. "So what do you say?"

"Oh, nonsense!" Astyages said, then closed his eyes again.

Bertkaameh stared at him angrily. "Why?" He asked.

Astyages looked at him. "They're only rules of thumb, two hammers hitting for three people, running to the end of the camp, climbing of a narrow wall that there's no way we can climb to the roof together at the same time..." Astyages allowed himself a wry smile. "You never make it!"

Bertkaameh stared at him defiantly. "We can make it through the darkness," he said.

"They have more knight at nights, did you know that?" Astyages said. "One of then is there, stood by the north balcony, hidden by the shadows. He's looking right at us."

Bertkaameh looked around spontaneously when he looked at Astyages again, he seemed to be sleep. "We need to get out of here, or we will die here inside!" He said, he looked disappointed.

"The plan has been well laid," Astyages said with closed eyes. "We can make it."

Bertkaameh stared at him. "But you say that's nonsense…," he said, confused

"We need a leader, and every slave must know about the plan," Astyages said, as he opened his eyes and sat.

"Are you nut?!! There's no way for all of us to escape from this camp," Bertkaameh grinned. "And I have to inform you that, sadly, one does not simply ascend to the position of leader," he said in an iron voice.

"We won't get all head for it together, but we start a revolt altogether." Astyages' eyes bore into him, sharp and bright as the points of swords. "Rebelling will buy the time we need, for three of us, whom the slaves had chosen, to escape," he said.

"Be hard for any man to risk his life especially to help a stranger to escape?" Bertkaameh said.

"They'll help us if we can activate our pledges," Astyages answered rapidly.

"What do you mean?"

"We'll back to attack Nineveh with the iron army."

"This is something that's never going to happen."

"This is something that you should not let others know," Astyages said, dryly.

"We have plenty of spies, we've been discovered," Bertkaameh said.

"First you need to make them silent," Astyages said.

"How?" Bertkaameh asked, hesitantly.

"The spies will be recognized by the fake news," Astyages said quietly. "If we kill a few, others keep silent."

"I never imagined you talk like this."

CHAPTER FIVE

CREEPING DAYS

Assyria, Nineveh, 627 BC, Winter

The slow days drifted on. Hara had grown used to waiting for days, and to being so patient. She had grown up in the king's palace, so she had learned to wait, like a full-grown tiger, for the right moment to attack.

"I'm not really in the talking mood right now," Yaafa said as soon as Hara entered. The day was warm and cloudless, the sky a deep blue. Yaafa was shaded beneath a canopy in the overlooking the river couch, one leg thrown negligently over the carved wooden arm of the bench. "I haven't slept at all, too tired even for talking," she said, scratching with dainty. "The great commander honored to have me as a guest in his house."

"All right, I got this; you have a lot of lovers. Do you want to know what I want to say, or don't you," Hara said in a bored tone.

"Speak like a woman of your age Hara," Yaafa said.

"You're going to help me or not?!" Hara snarled.

"I thought about your plan… imagine they really get married, well... what's the use? There's no point for me," Yaafa said. "That naughty girl will be the first lady of Assyria."

"You don't know your son?" Hara said, her voice dripping with sarcasm. "Sinshar is an inherently forgetful lover; he has gotten the infidelity from you and his father."

Yaafa's lips curl into a snarl, and Hara's eyes glazed over and continued. "Don't look at me like this… you fell in love at least once every week."

"It makes no matter," Yaafa said. "She will be the first lady of Assyria anyway!"

"She doesn't like you. She does not believe in our laws…" Hara cleared her throat; she looked uncomfortable, "like her father."

"I don't understand what you're getting out of this," Yaafa asked thoughtfully.

"All I want is respect and honor, what I had before," Hara said with a sullen voice.

Yaafa grinned. "You remind me your brother," she said as she was playing with her big ruby ring, "deceit, intrigue… these are your ways to obtain respect and honor." She stared at Hara. "I don't know why I trust you."

Hara was staring at her, with cold eyes. "Everyone has his own plans…" She sat beside Yaafa. "You trust me because you have no other choice," She grinned slyly at Yaafa. "Let's get back to our story; it's time to show our Semiramis to everyone. The celebration of the rebirth of the sun will be tomorrow evening, Mithra will be there, and she will present this year's sacrifice to God Marduk from the Semiramis imperial family. I want to show the people that we took second Semiramis to her own house… her presence with a red ornament of a court lady among the people will excite so much curiosity and comment."

Yaafa sat on the edge of her bench suddenly, overwhelmed with Hara's words. "You're out of your mind, this ceremony is significant to me, all eyes will be on me, and I won't let you ruin my night," she almost shouted.

Hara made a disgusted sound. "Seven bloody hells," she swore. "You don't get it, do you?… Don't worry; people will remember your beauty after this again."

"That's... that's not what I meant," Yaafa said irritated. "She has no idea how she behaves like a lady, and besides, what if she escapes?"

"A court lady will come to your palace, and she'll tell her in detail what to do and how to do it," Hara said, "and she won't escape."

"How do you know?" Yaafa asked suspiciously.

"Surely you don't expect me to make the same mistake twice." Hara got up. "I'll keep some little secrets to myself," she said, smiling, and left Yaafa alone.

Yaafa's emerald eyes escorted her, full of hate and bitterness.

*****

The slow days drifted on.

The creepy days were too tedious to bear.

Mithra was stepping on a flat part of the ground, among the Maple, elm, and poplar trees, which were partly cut down. Green leaves, yellow leaves, red leaves, it was a rainbow of vibrant, autumnal colors. The air was freshest after a rainfall, and the water drops from the red leaves continued to fall. The sound of running water in the river had a relaxing, hypnotic quality. She stepped off the path, into the rough grass and felt the squelch of the mud beneath. The water rises up and runs between her toes. She breathed deeply in the fresh air, smelling of pine and moss and cold.

Only Mithra could see those beyond the palm trees, in her dreams.

A beautiful young brunette woman stepped firmly towards the bed, bowed her head and put a gold tray on the couch, fixing her eyes on it.

"You can imagine it's the altar," a young maid of court, standing at the corner of the room said, arrogantly. "Keep in mind, never turn your back on the altar."

She had to learn many things, the toughest was being patient. She glanced at the young woman and then turned to the window. Savrina wanted to translate the woman's words, but Hara's sound interrupted her.

"Watch and learn!" Hara said, imperiously. "You have to learn how to offer your sacrifice to God Marduk." She stared at Mithra with a sullen face.

"I don't believe in your gods," Mithra said dryly.

Hara got up instantly. "Leave us!" She shouted, and the young woman left the room hastily. Hara went to Mithra. She was staring into the distance, ignoring her.

"You don't believe our gods," Hara stood in front of her. "So, you should pray to your god, may your GOD help your slave lover."

Mithra turned to her sharply.

"Don't look at me like that," Hara said. "I ask you to try keeping your arm straight, look at the altar and put the tray on it, that's all, nothing more."

"How do I know that? How do I know, when your damn wishes are going to end?" Mithra stood, staring into Hara, her eyes burning like the Nineveh's sun. "It's better to die than to be in a most embarrassing position, even for him."

Aggressive, and impolitic, who remain proud and fierce even in hell, like your mother, Hara thought, you might have the others fooled by your angriest glower, but not me. Hara gave no sign of her discomfiture but only smiled. "Our friendship must change into a calmer sort of goodwill," she said. "So, let me make a deal…" Hara hesitated, long enough to make Mithra curious. "Do what I ask… and in exchange, I will arrange a meeting with him!" Hara looked directly at her. Mithra's eyes lit with desire, an eager was filling her face. Hara continued. "He… what was his name? Yeah, Astyages… Astyages and you, alone." She laughed. "So you see, I've even known his name."

"How do I trust you?" Mithra said, her face glowering suspicion.

Hara grinned, went to the couch, and stroked the bloody red silk dress on it. "This color suited your mother best," she said, coughing slightly.

"That doesn't answer my question," Mithra said.

Hara glanced at her, smiling. "You can not trust me." She went to the door and opened it. "But you can wait." She went out and the door locked.

*****

The slow days drifted on.

Sin-Etli was not so sure things have gone well.

He could not do all this work on his own!

The court supports me, he thought, but they don't know me as anything other than a nominal king.

The sun was setting.

The yellow ball of fire changed to hues of orange. The sun cast its golden rays down upon the waves of the river, turning them fire red. The warm air brought salt to the lips, the boats were scattered over the harbor like fall leaves in a pond. *No music could be more beautiful than the sounds of the paddle splashes*, Etli thought.

The huge black granite temple of Marduk like a cold-blooded monster was standing on the riverbed. There were hundreds of girls, dressed in their most beautiful red dress, dancing around the temple, red poppies dancing with the relaxing waves of harp and lute.

Every year at this time, the Assyrian young women, rich and poor, beautiful or ugly, from around Assyria, came to this temple to ask their dreams from God Marduk: a bold, brilliant, wiry husband and many sons.

Etli hated this ceremony. He hated whatever forced him spent time with the courtiers. They will give him nothing but flattery and lies; he had never enjoyed living in court. On the other hand, he knew he was not someone who beloved of the court, he owed his throne to his greedy, drunkards, and revilers elder brother. It was weird; the great king had only two sons, although he has many women in his life. Sinshar had lived in the way that the great king could not announce him as the next king, and the courtiers had no choice but Etli.

Etli was never interested in the throne. He did not behave or talk like the rest Assyrian men. The courtiers used to admire the men with harsh tongues and violent behavior. The Assyrian men were great warriors, fierce and bold, who was enjoying war, women, and wine but Etli was a subtle man, wrote poems, and loved music. Music was a bridge between the earth and heaven for him. He was not interested in sitting on the throne, but he had learned from childhood, his goal in life should be in harmony with his country purposes!

Etli leaned back and stroked his long-thin beard. Even his face was not similar to the other Assyrian men; he has a yellowish skin tone, thin hair, and long, narrow eyes, sloping downwards to the nose, which could not be large and attractive like the Assyrian men even with applying kohl. He glanced at his mother between the royal women. Etli had gotten his face from his mother, a princess from Nisa.

Sara, his mother, was a captured princess when the great king conquered Nisa's army and occupied the East. It was traditional that the king first bedded the dethroned king's daughter and after that, the commanders could sleep with her, but the king fell in love with this shy and timid girl with almond eyes, and she became one of the most beloved women in the great king Haram. The great king always liked her best, even more than Yaafa, but in his old age when he was too old for wine and kisses and needed a women's kindness and love, Sara was the only woman who had the right to live in the great king's palace.

Etli gazed at the river, as the sun slowly sank beneath the horizon, his face showed no emotion. The music soared through the air like an eagle on an up-draft, taking with it the very souls of the listening audience. There was a lot of drinking and dancing, the moment of ultimate of the ceremony but some of the courtiers and senior officials still did not attend the ceremony. Such a thing had never occurred before, in the time of Great King, but now the courtiers and the army commanders got every chance to show their solidarity against the king's antiwar ideas.

In his father's day, the Assyrian Empire was at the apex of its power, but now, the civil war had weakened them. Many of the under Assyrian's control lands did not pay their tax, so there is not enough gold and silver in the royal treasury. Since the day that he was crowned they had no great war, and now, all the courtiers knew their king was a pacifist, so he was not interested in the war in any way. They believed that the new king's decisions definitely had made Assyria's power reduced. That is why the courtiers envied his father's royal manhood and the great Empire's glory.

Etli believed in peace from the very beginning. The peace would give them the opportunity to quell the insurgents, to forge the new alliances and to regain power. He had said repeatedly that their violence now was their weakness. Assyria had made hatred so much stronger than fear.

Sinshar was the king of Assyria without the slightest hesitation if Yaafa did not have her evil reputation, but she was famous for her illicit relations and even many of the ordinary Assyrians people said that Sinshar was not the great king's real son. Sinshar had full qualifications of an Assyrian popular king, he was a brave and strong warrior, but unfortunately he had gone her mother's way while Assyria needed a king who had the support of all the courtiers; otherwise, he could not overcome all the country difficulties, still caused major internal clashes.

Etli was grown tired of the myths. At the begging of his reign, he hoped that the courtiers realized the situation, but they were thinking of nothing but using trickery to gain more power.

Etli, the king of Assyria, looked at the people who were dancing, wished was there, one of them, danced without concern, drank wine without fear of being poisoned, and the end of the night fucked a girl without fear of a spy bitch. He sighed deeply in his chest and at the same time saw Arsen's tall, ungainly figure.

The chain around his neck swayed forward, propelled by the weight of gold, winged bull medallion. He runs his hand through his thin beard, rolled of thin woven golden strings. The king gave his Senior Minister a lingering look. Arsen was tall and bald as an egg. His face was so wrinkled that it was hard to tell his age, but Etli knew that he had been his father's Senior Minister for many years, and had even served his grandfather. Despite his age and girth, he was still nimble and smart enough, but so wily. His cloak billowing behind him as the wind came up, hid the man who stepped behind, although Etli didn't need to see him, he was Saber, a Median renegade commander who was almost everywhere with Arsen these days.

Arsen was his Senior Minister and also his most dangerous enemy.

Arsen had played an essential role in Etli sitting upon his throne. He wanted, actually, to get rid of a so stubborn, unreasonable, and the doggish bull king like Sinshar and replaced him with a gentle, submissive, even timid one but he found that he was mistaken very soon. Perhaps this was because Arsen never really knew Etli. Etli was very gentle and appeared more a poet than a politician, but he was at the same time stubborn, self-willed, and fastidious, and his manners, though well polite, were not pleasing. He had strange beliefs about his kingdom, and a strange ruling as King, regardless of what others thought. They found out they hate each other, but their political lives were tied together. Fire and ice, somehow existing together without destroying each other.

Arsen bent his knee, bowed his head.

"You're too late Lord Minister," the king said as he moved his hand slightly to allow him to release. "You lost the pleasure of seeing the young girls dance."

Arsen pressed his lips together; he did his best to ignore the king's irony voice.

"I always enjoy seeing young girls but serving my king is the highest honor for me, in fact, I'm here because my great enthusiasm to accompany my king," Arsen said. "I've no desire to be in this ceremony."

Arsen sat beside the king and Saber, with a handsome young man took the seats behind them.

The king was looking at the altar; the girls in long red dresses went forward and offered their sacrifices to find a perfect fate. *Believe in miracles is sweet more than enough that can ease the bitter taste of the truth,* Etli thought. "I admire your passion," the king said with a grin. "What is Lord Minister concerned about?"

"The king of Media has armed the Mannaean farmers as best he could with weapons from Media and Nisa; they are given months of training. He is organizing the fighting men into a strong company. Our two old enemies have combined against us, Media and Mannea," Arsen said.

"What do you expect, Arsen?" The king glanced at Arsen slowly. "We have been fighting with all countries and all peoples; a common enemy unites even the oldest of foes," he grinned, "Do you still think we should send soldiers and horses to war with other countries? How long do you think you can control them by warfare?"

"Your Majesty, with your permission, I should say yes," Arsen muttered, low under his breath, "I still think that the greater part of the world is mistaken about our power..."

"I feel just the way the greater part of the world does, Lord Minister." The King interrupted and said with a wicked light in his eyes. "It is time to defend ourselves; we must all understand that if we want to survive, we need to stop expanding our land."

"But if we show a waiting attitude, the Northman will attack at once." Arsen hesitated, then gathered up his courage. "And as you know, Your Majesty, our irony army had rescued our people from trouble many times in the past and would do so again..."

"Will you be able to bury the past?" The king kept his voice low, but Arsen could hear the fury in his tone. "The king of Medes has become a force to reckon in the last ten years if something provokes the king of Median... we could get into big trouble." He gave Arsen a baleful glance. "Especially without any warning!"

"No doubt by now you have received full information," Arsen said calmly. "One of our confederates was captured by them, and we have to go them to save him, but the Mannaean soldiers have lifted a sword against us."

"Do you take me for a fool?" The king said.

Arsen could see the tightness around the king's mouth. "If I have given offense, I am deeply sorry Your Majesty. All men know how much I love you, my King, and how much we need you but I told the truth."

"There's no offense higher than you've behaved as if you are the king," Etli sounded as angry as Arsen had ever heard him. "Perhaps you should remember you're not a king,"

"I will remember, your Majesty," Arsen said, frowning, as he bowed his head.

The king weighed his Minister long and carefully with his eyes and then stared at the stony stage, where the girls were dancing.

Arsen glowered at the altar, chewing his mustache. The twilight had faded to blackness. Arsen saw Yaafa in the flickering circle of lantern light, walking in a golden gown, mincing steps, and exquisite balance. At fifty-five, she still looked stunning, yet desirable, and that was what kept every man desires her and every woman hates her.

If you were not so goddamn beautiful, too much footloose, I dethrone this little snot today, Arsen thought bitterly. Hara loped silently beside Yaafa, like a ghost. Her pale face, her morbidly skinny body, her spider-like fingers, her awkward posture, and those strange immense eyes make her uniquely attractive. Arsen's attention just then was drawn in another direction.

Sinshar was following them; his hair had been pulled back tightly behind his head and fastened with a jeweled brooch. His stern look emphasized the hard, deep lines of his face. He rested his hand on the hilt of his sword; his braid was heavy with scented oil, woven with tiny gold chains. He was a head taller than the tallest man in the pavilion, but stepping light on his feet.

Arsen looked around; the pavilion was electrified. It took him a few seconds to realize that the crowd exciting was for a young woman beside Sinshar.

She was stepping towards the altar with pride and dignity, wearing a red dress, made of soft, satiny fabric, long and loose, slipped onto her shoulders, peppering her body with soft, sensual kisses. The lantern's light reflected off her olive skin, showing off her incredible beauty. She had a golden crown in her dark, warm red hair, a tiara just like the Great Semiramis' crown. Her eyes were more gold than brown. *Also like Semiramis,* Arsen thought, and a birthmark like a skull on the young woman's cheek drew all of his attention, *and ... the famous sign on Semiramis' face!* That took Arsen by surprise as if a statue of Semiramis had come alive.

The king who coldly ignored the royal's families entering even was staring at this woman.

Unlike the other Assyrian men who always walked one step ahead of the women, Sinshar was escorting the young woman respectfully. Sinshar stopped beside the stairs, waiting for her. She stepped forward, oblivious to the curious eyes, a puff of wind swept through her hair, she put her sacrifice on the altar and the glowing embers leaped and twirled in a fiery dance, twinkling like stars.

A gasp went up around the pavilion.

Mithra remembered the presentation process exactly, but she has so many other things to think about, her long skirt was in big trouble. She shifted her legs around under that skirt, took a backward step, but her feet slipped, and she lost her balance, her hands, reaching blindly out for something to catch her fall, she clutched at the altar.

No woman was allowed to touch the altar; everyone was feeling something terrible about to happen.

Mithra did not know what happened to people, but she drew back her hand unconsciously. There was nothing but silence in the pavilion, suddenly a bird with bright eyes and ink-stained wings seemed to float over to Mithra with the swift movement of the wings landed on the altar in front of her and cawed.

Again, the crowd stirred with murmuring.

Mithra took a look at the crowd. The color of the bird's eye was the same color as her. No one could even murmur. Mithra took a deep breath, she turned regardless of what she had learned and left the stony platform.

Etli felt a chill of fear; this was clearly a plot to do harm to his throne but this time more serious than ever.

"It's unbelievable."

Arsen's voice brought the king to his sense.

"I'm unable to know whether she is dream or alive," Arsen said in an excited voice.

The king could not find an answer, grinned and stared at the platform to nobody.

People love legends, but the one thing they love more than a legend is creating a legend. Very soon, everyone was talking about the young woman.

"She is Amitira's daughter, a descendant of Semiramis!"

"My mom used to say that Semiramis always lives at different times, different places, and different bodies."

"The fire burned redder than the stars when she came in."

"The fire flared up bright against her."

"I have fifty-six years old ... I've never seen anything like that."

"Did you see the crow? I've never seen a crow in Nineveh. What's that supposed to mean?"

"Have you heard? They said when Amitira fled to take refuge in our country, her Mannaean husband has killed her and the crows have to feed her daughter in the desert, just like Semiramis."

In the middle of the temple yard, ten virgin girls were dancing in bright colored clothes, with shedding rose's petals on the podium. Etli was staring at them, frowning, but he saw nothing. His afraid mind was struggling to figure out all the courtier's voices, but he found only bits and pieces of their words: Semiramis, glory, lost power, a new life ... but he was not sure if he found out those words or they are fake words that his afraid mind had made them.

He peeked around. He saw the young woman, sitting on the bench, looking at girls, seemed cold, proud, and indifferent. Her irresistible beauty, proud eyes, even that damn sign, everything was as they had seen during the years in Semiramis' status. *Who can, and why able to give life to a statue of Semiramis?* Etli thought, shaking his head as if he thought there was no getting over this.

Suddenly Sinshar turned his face, and their eyes met. He had kept his face in the shadow of the lampshade and had smiled in a peculiar way. He was the person who the courtiers wanted, brave, strong and militant. His eyes were soft by drinking wine steadily all afternoon, but it was not something that made the curt displeased. He obviously had learned his lessons well, although he was not a person who would rest beside his family.

Etli clenched her fists and gritted his teeth.

The music was thumping so hard. The crowd bones were vibrating as the dancer girls span rapidly, causing their long, flowing red skirt to plate around their waist and make a beautiful red rose, a buzz of excitement pulsed through the crowd. But Etli could just feel the anger, the fear, the frustration in his body and mind.

The king got up suddenly and went down the stairs. The music gradually faded to silence, everyone bowing on the knees before the king, shocked by his untimely exit from the ceremony.

Hara turned to the special royal seat, she wanted to determine whether Etli's reaction was equal to what she wished or not but she froze with widening eyes. Armaz was there, behind Etli, dressed in the Assyrian combat clothes.

"Armaz!" Hara said, her voice was quivering.

Hara was not the only one who stared at that young man, she felt Mithra took a deep breath and looked at the man heavily. She turned sharply and grabbed Mithra's wrist. "How do you know him?" she asked Mithra, her fingers digging into her skin.

Mithra had learned the Assyrians language enough to understand what she wanted to know, but she was shocked by her reaction. "Answer me, damn bitch!" Hara seemed terrible.

"My twin brother, Mahbod," Mithra said as she was looking at Hara surprisingly.

Arsen leaned heavily upon the huge royal seat, started playing with his blazon, according to his usual habit. He was smiling as if he was thinking about something pleasant.

"I know that girl very well," Saber whispered in his ear.

"Well, as if everyone has a mysterious story to tell today," Arsen said with a grin. "Come on, I'm excited to hear about her."

*****

The slow days drifted on.

His feet had grown hard with callus, he was finally getting used to sweltering heat, and each whip was not as painful as before.

The sickening smell of metal and blood blanketing the air in a choking aroma. The hot wind whipped around wildly. The victim was a young man with black hair and light brown eyes, his dull, gray skin was covered with insects that crawled up and down his stiff corpse. A torn cloth had tied over his mouth, and he was staring off into space, nobody could tell what he was staring at. He was cut open from the stomach, and the assailant left him there to die, the soldiers had found his body after four days beneath wood timbers.

The commander got the one glance at the body in front of him, instantly recognized him. This was the third spy, who has been killed this month. The commander turned to the slaves; they were looking at him, with bright eyes, something that made him afraid.

"Who did that?" The commander said, staring at them; no one answered. "Well, well, well, that's a good way to be...," he grinned, "but we don't have a slave alliance here." He raised his voice tone, "stop kicking me; otherwise you won't be alive!" He began to walk, through them.

"You!" The commander shouted; he was picking them.

"You!"

"You!"

The Commander stopped in front of Astyages, staring into his eyes, which were looking at him boldly. "I will teach you what slavery means!" He tapped with his daggers' halt on Astyages' chest several times. "My executioner prides himself on cleaving flesh from bone, with every swing." He passed him and shouted at the same time. "You!"

The Commander stood on a raised platform and shouted his orders. "One hundred sharp lashes and no food today!"

The Commander left them as he thought nothing could change those men in such a short time but hope. One of his soldiers came forward, a young palace guard was following him; they bowed.

"What's going on?" The commander snapped.

"They need two men to work at the garden in Lady Yaafa's Palace," the soldier said as he pointed to the palace guard.

"Send two men to them," the commander said.

"But Lady Hara has ordered him to take that slave," the soldier said hurryingly before the commander began to walk.

"Which one?" The commander asked curiously.

"The one who should be whipped," the soldier said.

"That Mannaean man, his name is Astyages," the palace guard said.

"The slaves have no name!" The commander took one step toward him and shouted. "Take another slave and say to your Lady that slave should be punished."

"It is not possible," the young guard said. "I request you to cooperate with me." He felt far from comfortable under the stare of the commander's keen eyes. "Lady Hara asked me to tell you, we don't want to trouble you."

The commander gave an angry sniff and stared at him in silence for a while. "Damned this court and its fucking sluts," the commander murmured. He heard a whoops followed by the snap of a whip. He looked at Astyages; his both hands were tied to the beam. The second lash landed on his shoulders, in one moment blood seeped from the wound and dripped down his back. He bit the inside of his cheek to hold a scream in, raised his head and strained his neck, stared into the eyes, which were concern about his reaction.

My weakness cause them to fail, Astyages thought, drawing air in his chest to calm herself, *I will never let you take hope from them.*

Another whiplash, and a shock, which spun his shoulder, and knocked him with a burning numbness in his elbow. He gave a gasp of pain but tried to remember sliding of Mithra's fingers on his shoulder skin so slowly, left deep warm and pleasant fingertips. She leaned in, so her forehead rested against his. They closed their eyes; their breaths were shaking. He could felt her slow harmonize movement on his body like a strange, unique dance…

"Enough!"

The commander's harsh voice brought him to his sense. The commander kicked Hooraan, who was crying beside the beam. "Keep your mouth shut or I'll shut it for you," he barked.

"Whip me instead of him," Hooraan said, crying.

The commander looked at him surprisingly, then slowly raised her eyes. "Untie him!" He ordered.

Hooraan was happy like a child; he thought the commander has taken his word for him. The soldier cut the ropes, and Astyages fell on the ground. Bertkaameh stepped forward to help him to get back on his feet. Astyages staggered to his friend and put out a hand to steady himself, his breathing was rapid and shallow, he raised his eyes and stared at the commander.

"If you keep this up, I'm going make that you wish never have these eyes which have stared at me," the commander said through his clenched teeth. He grabbed Astyages by his arm and dragged him to the palace guard. "Take him."

Astyages' eyes escorted him, surprisingly.

"What happened?" Bertkaameh said.

Astyages turned to him. "I don't know."

The young guard pointed to Astyages. "You!" He said what he had learned. "And you, come with me."

"Where?" Bertkaameh asked.

"Anywhere that I want to." He hesitated when he saw Bertkaameh's gazed eyes at him. "Lady Hara's Palace for work in the garden."

The guard walked out, Astyages and Bertkaameh followed him. The commander was looking at them through the window.

The guard took those two to the Nineveh's Bazaar. Even in the hot afternoon, there was a brisk business on the market. The vegetable hucksters yelled something in Assyrian, the children ran laughingly past each other, and the women were stirring the colorful fabrics, looking for the best deal. They passed them as Astyages eyes looked at them with pleasure, whatever smelled life make him excited.

"Who's Hara?" Astyages asked Bertkaameh as he inhaled the sweet smell of the apples from a vendors' cart.

Bertkaameh glanced at the guard, he was not looking after them, he was staring at the woman in the red dress with particularly large breasts. "The great king's younger sister, she was as rustles as the king, but after his death, she doesn't have any real authority," he laughed, "although it seems she is strong enough to save you."

Astyages nodded. "Yeah, but I don't know why." He turned his face and looked at the market that they had passed it with regret. "Why you said she is not as powerful as past?"

"The new king doesn't like her, actually I've heard the king requested that she keeps out her abnormally large nose out of his throne," Bertkaameh said laughingly.

"I never knew Etli was this stubborn, I've heard he is a poet gentleman," Astyages said.

"If he could he had replaced everyone who rebelled against him." Bertkaameh said as he wiped the sweat drops from his burning forehead, "but he doesn't enough popularity in the curt."

They had passed the houses made of mud and straw and walked through a wide road. On this side of the Nineveh, palm trees hung over the way and created a pleasant shadow. "Defiantly, the court prefers Sinshar, a wild and warrior man," Astyages said. "Isn't it strange that the court have borne this king and he has not to be poisoned yet?"

"Between these brothers, Etli has more lineage and support from people, even in the court, amongst all dissolute people in the curt, Sinshar is the worst," Bertkaameh said, "Dissolute would kill his brother if he could gain the court's trust."

They stopped before a large, rusty bronze gate, flanked on each side by a tall wall. Two huge Lamassu statues had stood above the palace gate. The weather is pretty mild into the beautiful garden that seemed endless. In the center, there was a pond as large as a small lake with flowering lily pads and a wooden bridge that crossed the middle. The flower beds were a riot of colors and even on close inspection, they were weed-free.

After a while, the guard stopped.

"Stay here!" The guard said.

"What we should do?" Bertkaameh asked.

"You will know," the guard said as he left them alone.

*****

Mithra was spinning around in front of the mirror. "How am I looking?" She asked.

She was most elegantly garbed in a beautiful dress from which trailed, according to their traditional style, a long white tunic, with a fringe border, which from the waist to the ankle fell in a curve,

138

and the fringe ended in some rows of pearls, and a rich embroidered mantle.

"Beautiful, so beautiful!" Savrina answered.

"No, that's not what I meant," Mithra growled. "Am I like the Assyrians women?"

Savrina shrugged. "It is an official local dress and your face…," she mumbled, "Everybody says, you look like Semiramis, you know."

"That's what I'm afraid of," Mithra sighed, "If he doesn't love me in these outfits…"

"He knew you have to do what they say," Sarina said, stroking her hair.

"I have one ominous feeling," Mithra said as she turned to the window. "When's he coming? What if she lied about this, huh?"

"It's not too late. Hara needs you so keeps her promise," Savrina said.

"You're right!" Mithra sighed. "From now on, I'll be her slave," she said as she went to the window and stared at the garden.

Savrina went on. "You have sorrows that shake your belief, try your patience," she said.

Suddenly Mithra grabbed Savrina's arm, her fingers digging into her skin. "He is here, right now, really," she said.

*****

Hara burned one stick of incense before the Shamashin's altar. She took a full step back and again bowed her knees. Hara came

139

to Shamash's altar in their private temple in the garden to be alone. She was in no mood for a conversation. She hated Yaafa, hated her pride, indecent behavior, and her madness for being more beautiful. *I've spent all my time with whom I hated them,* Hara thought. She was famous for her coldness, but no one knew how much she had loved love.

Hara's eyes twinkled gaily, and she pondered with a smile as she remembered the last night.

Finding him was easy.

Hara ran up the stairs in her hiding house in the suburbs, a smile on her face and a lantern in her hand. She put her hand on her chest, took a deep breath to calm herself and opened the door. He was there.

Mahbod turned to her. He looked nervous.

Hara's heart stopped in her chest. For a moment, she dared not breathe. The moonlight shone down on his face through the window. Hara's gaze fixed on his face, on his beautiful dark brown eyes, luminous with gentleness.

She was engaged in still the beatings of her heart.

"My Lady," Mahbod said as he bowed.

His words were like a warm touch on her heart. Hara closed her eyes with pleasure for a moment, when she opened them again, her heartbeat stronger. Hara stepped forward, shut the door and put the lantern on the table. She sat down on the bed stared at him. "Do you know why you're here?" Hara asked.

Mahbod seemed confused; he did not know what he should say unto her.

"You're here because I want to help you to start to live your dream life, that's all!" Hara said, smiling.

Mahbod managed a weak little smile. "I am yours to command, my Lady," he said, he looked calmer.

Hara got up, stepped forward. It was a dream, Mahbod was not a tough one like Armaz, but he looked just like him. She extended out her hand and started to earnestly caress his smooth fair skin, Mahbod inclined his head to look upon her pale face, quietly pleased when she slid down her fingers on his chest. He lowered his mouth, sucking her bottom lip into his mouth. Hara gave a soft moan.

"Fucking me is not easy!" She whispered against his neck, loving the brush of his stubble against her lips.

Mahbod laughed, "Try me my Lady!" His hand slid under her skirt, a millimeter from where she needed it to be.

Her fingers clenched in his hair to drag his head back. Her lips parted, and she allowed her teeth to nip at the line of his lower lip. Mahbod cried out in pain and Hara tasted his blood in her mouth, a small salty taste.

Hara opened her eyes, pleased with the memory of words, kisses, and passionate embraces. She took a handful of the frankincense powder from a silver jar and poured into the fire.

She stared up at the smoke that was curling toward the cloudless sky lazily and saw Shamashin's statue's ruby angry eyes. She knew the gods had rewarded her, the joy of revenge and the joy of love at the same time for all days that she had kept her hatred alive.

"I've brought him, my Lady!" The palace guard said.

Hara smiled. "Just do as I say!" She said.

*****

Bertkaameh threw a look at the palace. "We are not here for forced labor," he said. "I don't know what is going on and I'm worried about this."

"Yeah, I'm curious to know, why the lady of this palace has saved me," Astyages said as he was looking around.

"A woman is coming," Bertkaameh said, shading his eyes with his hand.

Astyages squinted his eyes against the sun and took a few steps closer to see well, and suddenly he began running, his heart was going faster than he was. He had forgotten his wounds, his heavy chains, and his ulcerated feet, he felt her in his arms, kissed her breathless, saw her smile, and heard her laugh.

Mithra cupped his face, looking at her anxiously. "You have grown thin!" Her eyes rolled forward onto Astyages' shoulder. "What are these wounds in your shoulders?" She said, caressing his skin, unable to get past a huge lump in her throat.

Astyages closed his eyes, her touch was gentle, warm and soothing but immediately opened eyes, fearing that he had seen her in his sleep. "You are so beautiful!" He said, as he kept looking at her with surprise. "You look like a real Assyrian princess."

"Yes, I am really an Assyrian princess."

Her words leaving Astyages in shock, he could hardly believe his ears. For a moment, he did not know what to say, he smiled, a nervous smile. "How's that possible?"

"I know this sounds kind of crazy, but this is my aunt palace," Mithra said.

"Yaafa? Don't tell me she's your aunt!" Astyages looked at Mithra's serious face, he grinned. "I've never thought I see you as an Assyrian princess... you were fortunate," he said, his tone was dry and the curve of his lips becoming ironic.

"What? Are you kidding me?" Mithra growled. "Yes, I'm here, and I've worn this ridiculous dress but look into my eyes; you can't see any luck in my eyes!"

Astyages felt he had gone too far. "Anyway, you're safe in your relatives' palace! It's perfect."

"As long as they need me," Mithra said. "I'm here for a reason, I am a descendant of Semiramis, and I exactly look like the Great Queen of Assyria."

Astyages' earnest face was suddenly transformed and grew serious. He looked at her thoughtfully. *Sinshar will kill his brother without hesitation if he could gain the court's trust,* Bertkaameh's words echoed in his mind. Everything was so damned obvious; Mithra could give Sinshar a new proof, which he needed so much. *He can bring back the popularity as a leader by a good marriage alliance with Mithra,* Astyages thought. Semiramis could seal the lips of Sinshar's enemies.

Mithra's voice brought him to his sense. "This could be the last time we meet together," she said. "Somehow I will run away, even at the expense of my life."

"Hush! Don't do anything stupid, just memorize everything I'll say," Astyages said as he cupped her face in his blistered fingers. "Three months later, on the full moon, come to the Nineveh's wall,

I was at the end of the labor camp, near the city, join me. We're going to run away together."

Mithra looked at him so blankly that Astyages think she has not understood anything at all.

"Be there, remember, the end of the labor camp, near the city," Astyages said. "Understood? Yes?"

"How do you imagine I do that?" Mithra said as the thought of her guards made her frown.

"I don't know, fight them, tricked them, do what you can but be there!" He said in haste as he saw the guard who was coming to them from the corner of his eyes.

Mithra nodded.

"I'm going to get you out of here. Just come out of the palace," Astyages said, his whisper fell into the silence. They stare at each other, deep into each other's eyes. His hand rested below her ear, his rough thumb caressing her cheek as their breaths mingled. He gently pressed a kiss into her palm with his hot lips, bowed his head and left her, too sad to speak.

*****

Midnight was creeping through the slave's camp slowly. The men's steady breathing was the only sound that was heard. Hooraan was sitting on the ground, building castles in the sand, and Astyages was staring at stars, lost in thoughts.

Bertkaameh sat beside him, quietly. He bent over to pick up one pebble, running his thumb over pebble's smooth surface. Astyages could hear his heavy breathing.

"If you want to say anything, don't hesitate," Astyages said, gazing at the sky.

Bertkaameh gave him a sullen glance. "I've been here for ten years," he said after a long silence. "I haven't seen my family for ten years. I've already lost my identity; I've not heard my name for ten years. I've forgotten respect, kindness, comfort…"

"I know what you going to say," Astyages said as he turned to look at him. "I live here, that means I know slavery. Don't worry, everything will be all right."

Bertkaameh looked at Hooraan, his fingers were clumsy, but his work was a perfect kind of handiwork.

"I know you love her but…"

Astyages interrupted him. "I'm not doing this because of love," he said, frowning. "Have you heard what she has said? There was only one way for Sinshar to win the throne, Mithra." His voice was trembling slightly, but he added. "Do you have any idea what this means? We must be prepared for the day that Sinshar unites Assyria and builds a great army. Sinshar will be engulfed our entire lands."

"Please don't hate me, but none of those matters right now for me," Bertkaameh said. "I just want to get out of this hell."

"I know, nothing is more important than our future to me and we are going to make it," Astyages said.

"But...," Bertkaameh said, he was restless, and he was rubbing the pebble with his calloused fingers.

"You trust me, right?" Astyages said.

Bertkaameh looked at him for a few moments and nodded. "I trust you like one of my own blood," he said.

"Well then, please know I'll never betray your trust."

He threw down the pebble. "It's going to be a tough road ahead, Astyages," he said.

Astyages grinned. "If anyone can do it," he squeezed his shoulder, "it's she."

*****

Mithra looked through the window. "Two watch guards were in front of my room's door and two under the window," she said in a low, furious voice. "They never leave one a moment's peace." Her fingers clenched pink and white around the white silk curtain. "Escape from this beautiful prison is impossible."

"My father said, impossible is a word which has meaning only for fools," Savrina said calmly as she was sewing a red silk gown for Mithra.

"Thank you," Mithra retorted. "He never said how to kill four guards with nothing?"

"Women kill men with their minds, not their hands," Savrina said.

"Your father said that?" Mithra asked.

"No, l got it when my father passed away," Savrina said.

"What is the meaning of that?" Mithra asked, curiously.

She gazed a long while at Mithra without answering. "The only way to get out of this beautiful prison is Sinshar," she finally said.

Mithra stopped before her in surprise, looking at her questioningly.

Savrina glanced at her and then stuck to her work again. "Make Sinshar fall in love with you," she said calmly. "He takes you out."

Mithra sat, frowning. "Are you out of your mind?" She leaned against the soft, chenille cushions, pretending she was not interested. "I've never been a charm, flirting woman!"

"You don't need a lot of effort," Savrina said.

Mithra looked at her. "No, I'm sorry, I can't do that," she said.

"Just remember what Astyages said." Savrina's eyes were fixing on Mithra.

Mithra turned her face. Fight them, tricked them, do what you can but be there, Astyages' words echoing in her ears. She sighed and lay on the bed, unable to soothe her troubled mind.

*****

The slow days drifted on.

Just a few months before, the days passed quite similar. He had been so engrossed with the job of getting his power back from his brother that he had paid little heed to what was going on in the world outside but things seemed so harsh these days. He was burning up with fever although he was never sick. He could not understand anything of what happened to him.

Sinshar could not take his eyes from her half-naked body and her graceful, sensual swaying motions. Samieh was a beautiful woman, she sang songs sweetly and performed dance beautifully, his mistress for more than a year.

He closed his eyes, hoping to sooth his feverish mind but the only thing that came to his mind was Mithra's beautiful face. Her beautiful eyes that were staring at him with proud, even hate. He was terrified of her vulnerable, hateful and angry eyes even in his thoughts. Sinshar imagined what her lips would taste like, at the same time, he felt the warmth of Samieh's naked body against him and quickly drove out the thought. He opened his eyes.

Samieh had a glass of dark red wine in her hand; she sat down. She tilted her head toward him. "My Lord is not pleased with my dance."

Sinshar wanted to take the glass, but she poured the wine over her body, slowly and lovingly. The narrow streams of wine flowed down on her breasts' pale skin. She took his palm and laid it on her breasts. He was staring at her wet nipples, and he felt his desire for her. Her eyes were a pool of waiting. Her breasts were small and perfect; he ran his hand lightly over her breasts, over the tender curve of her belly. She gasped slightly, biting her lower lip. He saw the tightness of her nipple, proud and erect. He felt trembled; drew back his hand immediately.

She grabbed his upper arm with one hand. "Please... My Lord."

Sinshar had thought he knew love well. Love was the desire for sexual pleasure with an attractive woman, it was one of the great joys of his life, and after that, he could back into his routine, manly life. However, this time he felt everything differently. Sinshar was restless; he could not stop thinking about her. Every time he closed his eyes, he saw her beautiful face again.

"Get out!" Sinshar whispered.

Samieh was laying down, naked; it was hard to be sure that she had heard aright.

"Get out!" Sinshar shouted at her.

She grabbed her clothes and run out of Sinshar's huge bedchamber. He was trembling. "Gods be damned," he roared. He wanted Mithra, with whole body and mind, the need of loving her was burning, more than fire. He grabbed the jar of water poured it over her head, yelling.

CHAPTER SIX

NEW SUN

Assyria, Nineveh, 626 BC, Spring

The expensive flowers were trampled under the hooves of his horse. He knew his mother would be mad but nothing mattered to him, and he was galloping through the beautiful garden. He did not know what had brought him here, his mother's steadily massages or his burning desire to see Mithra. To ease his mind, he looked away from the destroyed flowers, but he found himself surreptitiously glancing at her room's window, watching to see her. She was not behind there, and Sinshar sighed.

Sinshar slid down off the mare's back, hesitated, and stroked his horse's mane. He was furious for no specific reason. He overcame his lingering doubts, tied up the horse in front of the white marble stairs. A slave reached him, but Sinshar turned to him. "Don't touch her if you don't want she broke your bones under her hooves," he said.

Yaafa's maid of honor had risen and stood when he entered with bowed heads to greet. "My Lord," she said with a sullen face. "Please let me inform my Lady..."

Sinshar heard his mother's laughing, climbed the stairs regardless of the maid and pushed into the solar unannounced to find his mother laying on the bench. A very young man and Yaafa turned to him. The young man grabbed a sheet to cover his naked body.

"You fucking little rat, I might break your neck the first moment you tried to get in this palace," Sinshar said, disgusted.

The young man went out in haste right after hearing Sinshar's words.

"At least choose your lovers carefully," Sinshar said to his mother. He gave her a sour grin. "Are you interested in his character or his sex appeal?"

"I might break your neck the first moment you opened my bed chamber's door without permission," Yaafa said as she clambered out of bed and grab her robe.

"Why you send this massages constantly to me while you are too busy," Sinshar said as he watched his mother's beautiful body with wonder.

"You have chosen the wrong time for fun, kid," Yaafa growled, "You must attend the feasts with Mithra; the next one is in a couple of days."

"I've already told you, don't get me into this," Sinshar said, dryly.

Yaafa turned to him, her green eyes bright with the flame of her fury. "I won't lose this opportunity that Gods have provided for me," she shouted.

"I don't need your tricks," Sinshar said through his clenched teeth, "or as you said the God-given gift."

"Of course you do," Yaafa shouted at him.

"Mithra is not your slave; you can't force her to love me."

"My parents forced me to get married when I was sixteen, your father was fifty, and I have to inform you that I was not a slave."

"You are not Mithra, and I'm not my father, so I don't force her to get married to me," Sinshar said.

"What if she wants to marry you?"

Sinshar turned to the voice. There was Hara, standing at the doorway.

"That's impossible!" Sinshar said. "She has no reason to love me."

Yaafa grinned at his answer as she went to sit on the bench.

"How do you know that?" Hara asked.

"It's clear, her eyes blazing with anger and hate," Sinshar said.

"You've got that totally wrong," Hara advanced with a confident, sly smile as she leaned against the wall. "She will love you, I promise you," she said.

Sinshar's eyes escorted her; something was not the same in her. *Maybe a slight increase in weight that suits her,* he thought. He gave her a sour grin. "How would you plan to do that?" he asked, threatening.

"I'm not a witch son, I can't work miracles," Hara said, frowning. "But I know she has Assyrian royal blood in her veins. She can't hate you." Hara saw a hint of a smile on Sinshar's lips, which faded soon from sight.

"Just remember, you can't cheat me, you and l, we have made of the same soil," Sinshar said and went to the door.

"If that was true, you wouldn't be here right now," Hara mumbled when Sinshar closed the door.

Sinshar climbed down the stairs quickly, lost in his thoughts but in the hall gradually decreased the number of his steps. Mithra was there, creasing Sinshar's horse lovingly. It was the first time that he saw her smile and he just could not stop looking at her.

"It's strange," Sinshar said. "She wouldn't let anyone else hold her but me."

As soon as Mithra heard his voice, she subsided at once and her smile faded. Sinshar became penitent, but Mithra did not leave him, stood, stroking the horse's flowing red mane again.

"A stubborn horse feels love better than the patient one," Mithra was speaking Assyrian in a soft, sweet accent.

Sinshar stood silently. He preferred to look at her, trying to remember all these moments.

"I had a horse, as white as a pearl." She smiled, a sad smile. "So I had called her Morvarid, means pearl. Everyone said she is stubborn, but she was a loyal horse." She turned to Sinshar, stared at him, without hate, for the first time. His heated blood rushing through his veins.

"Your soldiers captured her too," Mithra shrugged. "I don't know, perhaps somebody cares for her more than me now." she flinched away from his gaze and stepped lightly away from him, following by a guard.

*****

She found a quite strange face when she looked at the mirror. She had long velvet robe draped over herself and a golden crown sitting atop her head. Mithra's dark red wavy hair fell past her shoulders, and the kohl had made her golden eyes, bigger and more attractive.

"She's not me!" Mithra said sullenly.

"Hey, remember our deal and don't let us grumble." Savrina was behind her, preparing her hair's waves. "Just be patient, it won't take long," she said.

"Short or long, it makes no difference… I'm going lost myself here," Mithra said. "I'm changing. I can feel it."

"Maybe it's not such a bad thing," Savrina said laughingly but when saw Mithra's sullen face, added seriously. "Don't make a big deal about it; you're going to a party, that's all."

"It feels kind of like I'm betraying my people in Mannea right now," Mithra said, tears shining in her eyes.

"Stop it Mithra, if you want to be free again … did you heard me?" Savrina said.

"Hush, listen," Mithra said, her voice quiet.

"What's happening? Is something wrong?" Savrina asked.

"Can you hear the whinny of a horse?" Mithra said.

"A…h, yeah the horses got tired of waiting…"

But Mithra was not there anymore; she rushed to the door and opened it. "Take me out." The Guard had not any choice, Mithra was running through the stares.

Morvarid was more restless than before; Mithra ran into the garden and put her arms around Morvarid's neck, swung on her neck. She laughed, cried, rubbing her face on her white brighten skin. The horse was quiet in her arms, she was snorting slowly, and her neck's movement was stroking Mithra's face.

She glanced up at Sinshar's face who was smiling joyfully. "How did you find her?" She asked, the tears were running down her cheeks now.

"It wasn't hard, in the royal stable everybody knows her," Sinshar said as he was going to her slowly. "To be honest, it cheered them to know that I want to buy her." He stood beside Mithra, her perfume and warmth of her body made his blood boil. "No one could get ride her!" He said quietly, trying to hide his feeling.

"You have no idea how happy I am to see her!" Mithra said. She was looking at him gratefully.

"You don't even have to say it," Sinshar said. He took the rein of his horse. "What are you waiting for, get on, today you don't need the carriage, mount and come along with me."

They raced past at a gallop, hallooing to the gatehouse. This was the first time Hara could hear the sound of Mithra's soft laughter, she grinned. "Go with them, Keep an eye on her," she said to a soldier who had stood behind her, as she saw at them through the window. The soldier bowed and got out heisted.

*****

She put a bite of roasted lamb's testicles in her mouth, one of Sareh, one of the most famous of court Ladies, innovative recipes that surprised her guests. *Its taste is good,* Mithra thought.

"Doesn't taste like semen?" Sinshar said, laughing.

Mithra made the most disgusted face, drank a cup of red wine to wash her mouth. The wine was sweetened with honey, with just enough of the poppy to make the guests happy that made Mithra dizzy.

Mithra turned Sinshar. "That was a bad joke," She said as she drained the drops of wine from her glass and reached for another.

I guess I'm drinking too much, Mithra thought. She saw Yaafa out of the corner of her eye. She could feel the fury in her green-eye. These days, Mithra was an Assyrian princess who they desired. *Maybe a little bit drunker than they wanted,* Mithra thought and laughed aloud. Sinshar laughed with her, he did not know what had made her laugh, but it did not matter, Sinshar loved everything in her. Mithra turned her back to her aunt, sipping her wine and admiring the dancers.

A dozen young women were dancing, around a man who was playing a pear-shaped lute; their finger cymbals added a nice ching sound in tune with the music. Every movement of the dancer girls was full of poetry. Their costumes were colorful, flowing garments, accented with flowing scarves and veils. They were moving their body in sensuous patterns, weaving together the entire feminine form. Their arms waving from side to side above their heads, their heads swaying, their garments fluttering, their veils hiding. Their features, yet seeming to show glimpses of dark, flashing eyes beyond.

A dark-haired girl, half naked, pivoted in a revolving whirl of sharp precision and perfect grace, her little bells around her firm breast ringing.

In Mannea, that sexual immorality was a sin against God, but for Assyrians, love and sexual expression often showed their respect and honor to their Gods.

The beautiful young women came forward, her dark eyebrows that almost met in the center, her eyelids painted dark blue by azurite, to being regarded as immoral and seductive. She was bringing a golden jar of milk and honey, hit the dance floor like a whirlwind, spinning, twisting, and gyrating. She knelt in front of the man, poured the mixed milk over his cock, the symbol of the power of Gods; she slid her fingers on his skin, slowly, rhythmically, and respectfully. His cock erected in her tattooed fingers.

"The basic principle of penis pray is that women possess more spiritual energy than men, and a man could achieve the realization of the divinity only through sexual and emotional union with a woman."

Mithra heard Sinshar's voice just behind her ear, smelt his heavy scent of floral oil perfume and felt his hot breath. She could hear the blood pumping in her ears. "I need some fresh air," she said as she got up. She rushed to the wide balcony, into the shadows, out of sight, leaned against the marble columns, and closed her eyes, panting heavily.

"Are you alright?"

Mithra turned; Sinshar was there, concern for her. "I'm alright," she said. "I guess I'm drunk so much," she grinned, hoping to hide her feelings behind a lie. She stared at the ground and shuffled her feet. "I don't belong here. I don't belong in your world. I don't really know how to be a princess."

"You know, the people like you just the way you are," Sinshar said, his eyes glittered with admiration.

Mithra gave a shake of her head. "I even don't want anyone to see me in this dress." She pointed at her creamy pearl gown, its sheets of the silk slipped onto her shoulders with the blowing of the night breeze, peppering her body with soft kisses.

Sinshar smiled, leaned forward and blew out her bedside candles, darkness covered them like a soft, familiar blanket. He moved his head closer to Mithra. "No one sees us now," he said.

She stood frozen, from both fear and excitement.

"I love you," Sinshar's words were smothered on her lips, devouring her mouth with a kiss. He kissed her madly, panting and out of breath. Mithra's mind commended violently to run away, her body disobeyed, and she did not flinch; instead, her fingers grabbed him so hard that they hurt.

He could taste the wine on her lips, and feel her small firm breasts pressed against him. "I love you," Sinshar said again.

"I...!" Mithra looked at Sinshar's eyes, dark with want, she swallowed, "I... I'll come to your palace," she said.

"I'll tell them now to make a litter to carry you," Sinshar said hurryingly.

"No!" Mithra said immediately as she grabbed his sleeve. "Not tonight!"

Sinshar looked surprised. "Why not?"

Mithra stared at his full, wet lips, swallowed again. "I don't know."

"All right! You can play as you want." Sinshar took a deep breath. "I'll wait for however long you want."

"One week, when the moon is full." Mithra looked at Sinshar's shocked face and added. "Don't ask why!"

Sinshar shook his head. "I don't ask, whenever you want."

Mithra licked her lips as if she would savor the sweet taste of his lips on hers. "I want to get out of here," she said nervously. "Take me home please!"

Sinshar caught Arsen's face staring at them from the window before he went off obediently with Mithra's arm in arm.

*****

Mithra stood and stared at herself.

The mirror showed her a young Assyrian princess, a living statue of Semiramis as Assyria saw her. In Assyria, everyone used to see her, in the dress of Queen Semiramis, a tunic with long sleeves. Her shawl wrapped once around her lower body, covering the lower part of her tunic then wound up and around her upper body, draped over her shoulder. He wore her hair decoration too, a precious metal tiara on her short waved dark red hair, which made her look exactly like the famed queen, Semiramis. She was beautiful, talked but little, with a little bit of mystery. Besides, she had a huge story that had gotten her well famous. Sinshar was right, the Assyrian people liked her just the way she was, with her dark skin, keen eyes, often-sullen face, and her birthmark, looked like a skull on her cheek, the same things that because of them she was rejected in Mannea.

She was an Assyrian popular princess for almost one year and today was the last day.

She looked at herself. All she saw was her dark red hair, sullen face and golden eyes still looking at her but in inside, she had a firework of different emotions, rage, love, frustrations, proud and fear. She ran a finger over the frame of the mirror, feeling its cool ridges and grooves. She felt as though just roused out of sleep.

"Are you sure there's a full moon?!" Mithra asked Savrina in a low voice.

"A full moon has lighted most of the garden, though the drifting clouds have created the stretched shadows," Savrina said as she walked twice around her, adjusting the folds of the dress with her hand. "Don't worry because there's no need of it."

"Then why do I have this weird sinking feeling?" Mithra said, as she put her hand on her chest, trying to keep calm but her heart was fluttering in her chest.

"Sit down for a second and take a deep breath," Savrina said. "Everything's fine."

Mithra boldly snatched up her golden flowered skirts, oblivious to Savrina walked forward a few steps, and glanced out the window. The fog grew thicker, shimmering upon the garden. Above, the full moon, silver, and bright could not be hidden behind the creeping gray clouds, and shone intimidatingly on the land beneath, like the eye of the devil. It won't be long now before midnight, she judged from the black outside the window.

Mithra turned to Savrina. "I do wish you could come with me tonight," she said, not for the first time that day.

"Don't worry about me." Savrina smiled sadly. "I'm just really going to miss you."

"It's so hard to leave you..." Mithra turned her head away, to hide the first tear. "If I survive, I will always remember you."

She felt Savrina's hand on her shoulder; she whirled and saw her eyes full of tears. "I'm sure you'll be home soon."

"I'm afraid, just..." Mithra drew from her pocket a small bottle. "Just everything seems more than simple."

"Don't worry," Savrina said. Mithra thought how many times she had heard that today.

"Only a few drops." Savrina added and managed a wan smile, "then Sinshar should sleep for a week."

"If he lied... what if Sinshar isn't alone?" Mithra said thoughtfully.

Savrina stroked her fingers reassuringly. "Don't worry! There's no one but him."

"How do you know?"

Savrina let Mithra's hand drop. "Arrangements have been made...," she said discomposed by her questions.

"Who?" Mithra said, shocked.

"What do you mean?" Asked Savrina, bewildered.

"You said, arrangements have been made... who? Who made the arrangements?"

Savrina chewed her lip and tried to move away from her, but Mithra backed her into a wall, pressing her hands against her shoulders. "Who?"

"You know what I meant, Sinshar... Sinshar has made the arrangements."

Mithra released her. "You're lying!" She gave him a sour grin. "You're lying!"

Mithra went to her bed, heavyset, shambling. "Where'd you get this bottle?" She remembered suddenly. "You said you snagged it from Yaafa's medicines, was that another lie?"

Savrina looked at her, red-faced, struggled for breath.

"Who asked you to do that? Yaafa?" Mithra said quietly. Her voice sounded as if she might cry at any instant.

A knock at the door was heard, Yesna, Jamaspa's mother, stood in the doorway. She didn't need to observe court formalities here, she felt Mithra like one of her grandchild.

"Hara asked you are ready or not?" Yesna asked.

"I'm not going anywhere tonight!" Mithra said felt a lump in her throat

"All right, all right! Hara has been planned this," Savrina said hastily, "but she means well. If she saved your mother and father, she can save you too."

"She didn't do it!" Yesna said as she sat on the bench calmly. "I heard about Amitira's story from Yaafa, with convincing details, Yaafa has saved her sister."

"But what makes you affirm so confidently and emphatically that it's not she?" Savrina growled.

"Maybe Yaafa has done some good thing sometimes but Hara, never! Lying is her way," the old woman grinned. "I guess she has promised you that you free you after that."

Savrina said nothing but her face betrayed her.

Yesna smiled. "Nobody would be allowed to release a captive, even Hara," she said.

Mithra could taste bile at the back of her throat. The story was so hideous she suspected it had to be true.

She rolled the small bottle between her fingers. "Three months... three months I was trifled with you. Hara has gotten much fun on my foolishness!" she turned to Savrina; Savrina had never seen her eyes so full of anger. "Your father didn't tell you, liars cannot be trusted."

"It's not possible that she lied," Savrina said, quietly.

"What's in your hand?" Yesna asked.

Mithra glanced at her then stared at the bottle again. "An unconscionable lie, a medicine that I imagined will put Sinshar on the bed, only in a few moments."

"Give it to me!" Yesna asked.

Mithra handed her the bottle; she looked puzzled. Yesna downed half of the medicine. "Let's see what happens," she said.

After five minutes, Yesna had sat there yet, with no signs of sleepiness.

For a long time, Mithra did not speak. The only sound was their breathing. "It all seems clear enough to me! We are being fooled by her," she said at last, in a heavy wooden voice.

Yesna gave her a pitying look. "You are not going to let yourself be sad." She took both of her hands to hold. "You can still find a way to escape."

Mithra shook her head. "They know all about us," she said, tears filled her eyes. "The end of the labor camp, near the city…" She had to bite her lip to keep from sobbing. "Astyages will be there tonight, waiting for me… where he will be killed, which my fault will give to him."

Yesna lowered her eyes. "I know every room and path in this house. You know, if the guards were not here I could take you there easily, and you could reach him before they discover you."

Savrina had hidden her shame behind a sullen look and a face blank as a slate. "If Mithra was not here, the guards won't be there." She said, in a low voice.

Mithra and Yesna exchanged looks of surprise.

*****

Yaafa waved the peacock feather fan gravely. "Good Gods, only get it over soon!" She said.

The night was windy, with the stars hardly visible through the scuttling clouds. The wind whispered through the tall arched window, sharp with the smell of the river. Hara was watching two guards from the window, who were ready in the garden to escort Mithra to Sinshar's palace. "What do you mean by that?" She asked Yaafa. "We can't end the party when the real fun is about to begin."

This night must be too long, as long as that night that Amitira declared her love for me, Hara thought, after being fucked with fury and losing her lover, my vengeance will be complete.

"You foolish girl, she had thought she is free to act whatever she wanted." Hara stared into the darkness of her opponent, coughing. "Your fucking fate is awaited you between the Sinshar's bed sheets, selfish bitch."

Yaafa made a disgusted face. "How can you say such things?!"

Hara passed off Yaafa's sulky question with a laugh and sat down to rest.

"How did you announced the labor camp's lord commander about that boy's plan?" Yaafa asked another question irritability.

"He has no idea what will happen this night," Hara said.

Yaafa dropped the fan at once and stared with an appearance of wonder and perplexity at Hara. "Have you lost your mind? What are you saying?"

"Do not worry honey, wind's in our favor," Hara glanced at her and smiled. "He's dead anyway if his escape plan fails and Mithra could forget him, and if he succeeds, the entire blame will be on King Etli because he will be the only king that in his kingdom a slave succeeds to escape."

"You are like a deadly coiled snake, dangerous." Yaafa raised an eyebrow. "I don't understand how I can trust you for one minute after all these things."

Hara laughed, her laughing mingled with the deeper voice of coughing. "You will trust me, as long as you need me."

"I must be careful because I don't want to go with you anymore, especially..." Her green eyes narrowed in suspicion and looked at her beautiful blue navy robe and her well-dressed hair. "Especially these days that your mood is in a better place!" She got up. "I couldn't bear it anymore. I need to be alone in my bedchamber."

Hara dropped her eyes; Mithra was about to step up to the carriage. "You must be prepared for anything bitch," she whispered.

*****

Sinshar gave Arsen a cold look and frowned. He did not listen to him. Arsen was gossiping about the latest news, of the newly bestowed honors and the changes in the positions of the court functionaries and did not care Sinshar was hearing it or not.

Sinshar's expression was particularly sour. He did not want to ruin his most lovely night by a conversation with Arsen.

"Look," Sinshar interrupted. "Get to the point already, if you have one, Lord Minister."

"You're in a grim mood son," Arsen raised an eyebrow, "but I thought I have a juicy story to share with you."

"I've been in a grim mood for a very long time."

Arsen smiled. "I had thought you preferred frankness, Your Grace."

"Lord Minister, may I speak frankly?"

"I seem unable to stop you," Arsen said, his brown eyes rested on him sardonically.

Sinshar leaned forward with a sour smile. "All people knew it that you had done a great deal to secure the success of that coward."

Arsen leaned back in his chair. "You've got that totally wrong," he said in a sulky, sullen tone. "YOU had done a great deal to secure the success of that coward when you lived differently from the way I had done."

Arsen was staring at Sinshar.

Sinshar's eyes hardened at his words, he stared down at the table and said nothing.

Arsen's hair is grey, and his face lined, but he still could break me with his tongue, Sinshar thought. He raised his eyes slowly. "You expect me to believe you came here, at midnight, alone, to blame me about my past!"

Arsen smiled. "It is quite the contrary; I came to talk about the future, about how we can stop repeating our past mistakes."

"I'm listening, but say nothing in the way of blame or praise," Sinshar murmured, raising his eyebrows at Arsen. "I hate to sound like a peevish child tonight."

Arsen grinned. "All right! I'll talk briefly and frankly." He took his heavy gold medallion in the shape of a winged bull, his family crest in his hand as he always did while he had an important idea in his head. "These things are of the past, and everything is different now. The people don't really care about your past at all now; they prefer fairy tales. It is the fatal nature of this people to substitute a phantom for reality. Today, from the north to the south, people whisper their fantasies together as actual happenings."

"And if it wasn't, we wouldn't be here sharing this quality time together, now would we?" Sinshar said as sipped his wine, triumphantly.

The old man hesitated. His wrinkled hand stroked his gold medallion. "You said you don't like to listen to blames but I guess you never minded saying them."

Sinshar pushed his fingers into his hair and made a furious face. "Gods, you've been my friend since I was a kid and you sold and dishonored me because of the guy who does not deserve to live in Great Assyria, let alone take possession of its king."

"I'm just thinking about Assyria," Arsen said, his voice sounded angry. "Assyria must survive no matter who holds the throne, and I must enthrone who have the strength well enough to hold the dreadful dragging weight of the throne."

Sinshar's face turned red. "Who is that man? Etli?!" He almost shouted.

"No," Arsen barked. "I can tell you're the right person for the job but when everyone says so. This is what we didn't have before but… but now thanks to your female supporters' talent, we could have a dream-come-true life… but,"

Sinshar's golden eyes narrowed in suspicion "But what?" He asked.

Arsen poured himself a cup of wine and drank it down, hoping to calm him. "Tales are always told in my country in the very way I am telling," he said. "In Assyria, King rules by a sort of mesmeric fear, which you have it in your hands now: your Semiramis, with all tales of levitation that the people are building around her."

"Her name is Mithra!" Sinshar said coldly.

"I prefer her Assyrian name...," Arsen studied Sinshar's face for a long moment before he said, "... and I hope she stays that way."

Sinshar gave an angry glance out of the corner of his eye. "If you want to tell me something, say it frankly before I really get mad."

Arsen looked straight at him, his dark eyes determined, even defiant, but on his lips was seen uncertainty. "I have a friend who's like a brother to me," he said at last.

Sinshar's eyes were still suspicious. "That short, ugly man with an unpleasant voice," he said. "I don't know how you're enduring him; I hate traitors even if he was traitor to the Median crown."

Arsen nodded. "I want to tell you something; after that, you may hate him so much more or like him."

Sinshar gave him a quizzical look. "What?"

"He's the one who has captured your Semiramis."

Sinshar laughed. "You were right, I'm not sure if now I'd like to break his neck or give him a reward."

"But that's not all," Arsen said. "Saber knows her very well, in fact, he told me this young woman has ruined all our plans to destroy the Median king alliance with the Mannaean tribes."

Sinshar's nervous laugh echoed through the hall. "Fucking liar!"

"He doesn't lie, there is unspoken evidence," Arsen said in a dangerously soft voice, then grew more serious. "She was engaged with one of the Median king's close relatives. The wedding date was set before the Assyrian army attack began, but they captured, together! The boy is in labor camp now." He didn't stop looking at Sinshar. "Maybe she's manipulating you."

Sinshar's hands clenched on the arms of his chair. "Tell me what the hell's going on in your damn head, Arsen?"

"I have only one idea in my damn head," Arsen said, stone-faced and glum. "I wish this girl would love to have you, so we could use this story that was going smoothly so far to our advantage so I'll be able to get rid of a useless and proud king." He leaned back, took a deep breath.

Sinshar got up and walked away from him. There flashed into his mind, the picture of Mithra, her kiss, he went toward the window overlooking the yard. "She doesn't lie to me!" He said and at the same time remembered that Mithra had never told him that she loves him.

Arsen warned him. "A woman has no weapon but her guile."

There was a sound of hoofs in the twisting stony path in the garden, and he saw a pale illumination of the lantern through the trees. A fire of pleasure melted his heart. Mithra had been cloaked and hooded as she stepped from the carriage, a white cloak embroidered in gold, an expensive gift from Sinshar.

Sinshar turned to Arsen. "She doesn't lie to me!" He said again in a firm voice.

"How do you know that?" Arsen's tone seemed to hint at doubts.

Sinshar smiled, let him read into that as much as he likes.

"Lord Minster, you're invited to our wedding ceremony next week. SEMIRAMIS and I are getting married because we are in love. Love changes everything." He went in front of Arsen. "I'll sit on my throne, with you or without you, and if you want to remain a part of that, I recommend you follow me not that ugly traitor. I guess I should leave you, I have a distinguished guest tonight." Sinshar took another step but turned suddenly as if he remembered something. "Say your friend, be quiet or I'll cut his tongue out."

Arsen nodded, he knew Sinshar is serious. Sinshar left. Arsen sat there in silence. He heard the distant his footsteps echoing off walls from outside. Now those old weasels have reasons to put trust in this girl, and everything was all in harmony. He could be convinced everything will turn to account when love is once set going.

*****

Sinshar climbed the winding stone steps, running as fast as his feet would take him. There was no one in the house, no guards, no servants, even no singers.

He stepped into the bedchamber with a glass ceiling. Mithra was there, sitting on the edge of a vast bed. The room was already a blaze of light, with torches burning in every sconce. The flickered moonlight painted her white cloak in shades of silver. Sinshar's heart throbbed. He had made the best provision for her. The floor was covered with colossal lion skin rugs, and servants had lit the sticks of incense to sweeten the air.

There were sweet cakes to eat and wine to drink. Sinshar poured two cups of wine. The windows were open, and he took a deep breath and filled his chest with the flowers fragrant from the balcony.

"I've prepared this room for you, a long time ago, when you first came Nineveh." He sat behind her, put down the goblets of wine beside her. "I had grown used to lie on the bed, trying to imagine what it would be like if you allow me to kiss you." He hesitated half a heartbeat, long enough for him to enjoy listening to her heavy breathing. "I prayed to the gods," he laughed softly, "for the first time… and…," he sighed, "and now, you're by my side."

Sinshar brushed his fingertips lightly on her spine, feeling her trembling body. *I was foolish to worry about making a mistake,* he thought. He grabbed the goblet of honey-spiced wine and take a deep swig. Sinshar put his hand beneath her chin and raised her head, to look in her eyes.

A clap of thunder rumbled in the distance, off to the east, the cloak slid off her face. The wind sighed through the chamber, and the flames gusted and swirled. Savrina raised her head to look up at him, her big black eyes shining in the flickered torch lights.

Sinshar drove back a step. "What the fuck are you doing in here, bitch?"

Savrina was so pale that she looked about to faint, but she said. "You never take her by force."

Sinshar felt as if he had been slapped. He tried to snatch a breath; his fury had no bounds. "Hussy bitch," he snarled at her. "Hussy bitch," he repeated, grabbing her throat with one hand and stabbed her to the wall. "Hussy bitch!" He kept saying it, over and over, until choked her.

Sinshar was running madly to the door, it was the last blurred image in Savrina's eyes and then she breathed her last.

Sinshar's terrible roars were echoing in the empty palace, unable to restrain his desperate anger. He ran through the hallway and down the twisting stairs. The gate opened and shut, and Hara stood in the doorway, looking at him. The smile faded from her face when she saw his face, replaced by a confused scowl. Sinshar stared at her with his awful eyes. He cried wrathfully and irritably, grabbed her arm and yanked her. "Where is Mithra?"

"Right here, I saw her when she was coming here…," Hara mumbled.

"You were wrong, like always," Sinshar said through clenched teeth, as he released her. "Her maid has come to me in secret, disguised."

Hara stared at him, wide-eyed, her breath tight in her throat. "Go to the Nineveh wall, at the end of the labor camp, near the city… hurry up."

Sinshar glanced at her; there was no time for questioning. He rushed to the door, leaving Hara perplexed behind him. As she stood there, she heard from the garden the noise of hoofs broke out, and gathering to a gallop, went hammering away into the darkness.

*****

It took just a few minutes for the fire to spread up the tower.

The labor camp was a place that looked an awful lot like hell. The stones were cracking and split, the fire devoured the pulleys' ropes in moments, and part of the upper walls fell away and landed with a crash that shook the camp, sending up a cloud of dust and smoke. As the wind rushed in through the broken walls, the fire surged upward. The soldiers were caught entirely by surprise with the fire. They had become confused and perplexed almost as much as the slaves had grown stronger, and more daring.

The hammer ranged, and the last heavy chain opened from his foot. Astyages threw the previous look at the Lord Commander who shoved his longsword through a slave's ribs before flames leaped into the sky, whirled around each other and made a wall of fire.

Astyages took Bertkaameh's hand and said, "Now is the time my friend. We have just twenty minutes, come on then," Bertkaameh nodded. They were running for the wall, as fast as their legs could carry them but as they put weight onto the first few steps, they realized their plan would not be so easy. They had to have tiny pauses between every attack of the soldiers until a dozen slaves come running to defend them. We have to go, Astyages reminded himself. At the end of the camp, near the fort, eight soldiers and a stout commander mopped their brow against the heat, lined up against them. There was no way past.

A thunder sounded very close.

The clouds raced across the moon's pale face. The wind was rising, and the fire surged upward. The flames leaped into the sky, whirled around the fort and rushed toward soldiers. A soldier, yelping with pain and shock, robbing his burning clothes to the ground and others had enough time to the slaves, and six of them gathered near Astyages and made a pact together to defend them.

Bertkaameh put out his hand blindly and felt broken rubble and beaten ash, by the drift of groping, found the cracks from the stone wall, and climbed out on to the wall. After him, Toma, their friend started to climb up the wall and then Astyages who watched everyone and everything around them.

The ashes tasted like freedom!

*****

The mist had thickened to a slow, cold drizzle.

They topped their way to the wall when noticed gleams of wildfires in the camp. Mithra needed only a few minutes to reach them. She drew near Yesna; she looked a little wistfully at her as she took her hand and held it. "You might never see me again…I have to go." Her eyes were filled with tears. "Thank you for being my grandmamma…"

Yesna interrupted her. "I come with you if the soldiers stop you, I can say you're my daughter!"

Mithra smiled, pointing with her head to the fire in camp. "All soldiers are in the camp, no one stops me."

Yesna stared at Mithra's eyes. A tear rolled down her wrinkled cheek, and she hugged Mithra tightly, "I know you don't believe my Gods, but they've made a miracle for my Jamaspa once… I stay here to pray to my ancestors for help."

"If I wake up tomorrow morning, I thank your Gods for the new day," Mithra whispered in her ears.

Mithra's footsteps echoed through the bare and stony path. The darkness swallowed her. The thunder crashed and boomed, and rain began to fall in crazy, chaotic drops. She turned to give Yesna one last look, there was a concern in her eyes as if she did not want her to go.

*****

Astyages' legs were seizing up with the effort to keep climbing. He mounted the stone wall on tiptoe, glided along the wall and scrambled to his feet immediately to look around. The only lights overall the stone roadway were the shining flames of fire that was burning throughout the labor. No one has seen or heard.

"Why are you just standing there?" Toma yelled from the other side of the roadway, under the palm trees.

Astyages looked at him and went to him with faltering steps.

"Come on, come on!" Toma yelled again, looking at the dark water, darker in the shadows of the clouds, which had covered the moon now. The river, swollen by the heavy rain, was waited for them. They heard the footsteps, growing louder, and after a few moments, Mithra emerged into the light, looking nervous. "Astyages." She cried, her voice shaking. She flew to him with open arms.

Astyages opened his arms and received her. "I'm glad you came baby!" He whispered in her ear.

Toma stared at the stranger. "Who is this you brought with you?"

"Toma, we must hurry!" Bertkaameh said, taking Toma by the arm and drawing him towards the river.

Toma wrenched her arm from Bertkaameh's hand. "That wasn't part of the deal," he said.

"I knew all about her," Bertkaameh said, abruptly. "We must leave this place, now!"

"You're mad," Toma sneered. "We should not lose this chance."

"We can make it." Astyages proceeded to walk toward the river, holding Mithra's hand. "There's no time to waste," he said.

Toma struck an open palm in Astyages' chest. "Bertkaameh, you and I will go, alone."

Astyages released Mithra's hand, reached up under Toma's jaw, and grasped his neck as if he meant to throttle him, but instead, he spoke... his voice was threatening. "We're all getting out of here, together!" He left him with a look that dared any man there to question her presence. He seized Mithra by the arm without a word and started toward the river with her.

"Wait!" Toma shouted.

Astyages stood a moment, looked at him uneasily.

"I go first," Toma said.

Astyages took a step backward. Toma walked quickly to the river, eyed them angrily as he passed. He dived, they heard a loud splashing, and he vanished into the black and cold water for a while. When he started to swim away, the rain was beating down even harder. Bertkaameh stepped forward, glanced at Astyages. Astyages nodded and wanted to dive, but at the same time, they heard Toma's horrible cry of pain. He was dragged into the water. After a few moments, he breaks the surface again, gulping at the air. His head was bobbing up and down; his terrible voice was full of horror. They were looking at him, fear to consume their face. Tension grew in Mithra's face and limbs, her breathing became more rapid, shallower. Something was moving through the green darkness of the water, something foul and horrible was hurtling toward Toma.

Bertkaameh gasped. "Gods have mercy, he's bleeding…" The words broke in his throat.

His head was dragged downwards, his long frightened cry faded to silence, and then all was still, as still as when you wake up in your bed in a dark room from a bizarre dream.

They were still keeping their eyes on the dark water's surface.

"What are you waiting for? They ate it all up."

A great gust of laughter went up from behind them, and they looked back.

They were four. The Lord Commander in front and three soldiers waited behind him, their black cloaks, blowing in the wind. Their faces were bright, by a burning torch in the hand of one of them. The Lord Commander had a triumph smile on his lips.

"You haven't heard what they say about the real knights of Nineveh?" He said to them. "They don't sleep! They are living into cold, deep, inscrutable darkness of intrigue, bloodshed, and come out only by rebel and deceiving spirits."

Then he went toward them wavy and graceful, looking at Mithra and her golden eyes, his lips falling into their habitual sarcastic smile. "You were as sure about that as you invited a guest!" His hand touched Mithra's face, her hair but she twisted away from him. The Lord Commander grabbed her hair and pressed a knife to her throat.

Astyages stepped on the Lord Commander, a soldier speeded in toward him. The soldier raised his sword, but Astyages grabbed a rock and bushed it aside with it. He knew the next thrust would be to his chest, so he pushed the other soldier toward the oncoming attack. The soldier dropped his sword and grabbed Astyages' throat. Another soldier smashed his sword's halt to his face. Astyages spat blood and fell in his knees.

Bertkaameh tried to go toward him, but the other soldier seized him. The breath went out of him; it was all he could do to gasp. The Lord Commander was staring at them, Mithra took advantage of his distraction butted him with her head and broke his lip. She snatched the dagger out of his hands. She circled, the blade of the dagger hissed against the Commander's cheek, missing his eye slit by an inch and cut a part of his ear. He cried in pain. Mithra turned him and glared at him.

"Wizards die the same as other men." The Lord Commander said, drawing his longsword. He looked her in the eyes before slid his sword into her belly.

"Noooooooooooooooo!"

"Noooooooooooooooo!"

Tow men shouted, Sinshar and Astyages so that their voice rang far through the darkness.

They heard footsteps, Sinshar running as fast as he could toward Mithra's bleeding body on the ground. He fell on his knees, trembling, as the Lord Commander and the soldiers had bowed. His arm went around her, perhaps with tears in his eyes, and embraced her. Sinshar picked Mithra up in his arms.

Their eyes met.

Astyages stared at Sinshar's eyes, startling likeness to Mithra's golden eyes.

Sinshar stared at Astyages. She was engaged with one of the Median king's close relatives. The wedding date was set before the Assyrian army attack began, but they captured, together! Arsen's voice echoed in his mind. He looked at Mithra, her chest was rising and falling with each shallow breath, her sightless eyes were looking at him. Sinshar could feel her warm blood running on his fingers.

"I don't want to, I cannot lose you," Sinshar whispered.

He took her in his arms and went to his horse, running, as Astyages' eyes were escorting them.

*****

The labor camp, the Great King's unfinished palace, had collapsed into smoking ruin. The fire damage was catastrophic so the rebel leaders would not escape the terrible execution of the king judgment upon them.

Nothing remained of the forte building but the stone foundation, charred black. The smoke still rose from the ashes. They had tied them in the forte's stable; the Lord Commander had commanded one of the tired soldiers to watch over them. After the last night, war, and chaos among the slaves, the soldiers who could remain there at their posts were few.

The only sound audible was the men heavy breathing, in the heavy air stank of smoke.

"I wish I could only die," Bertkaameh said, his head fell upon his chest.

Astyages found nothing to say, his eyes were fixed on the wall's thick beams of wood, blackened and charred from where the flames had licked at them.

"We have to sit in the tub."

"What's that supposed to mean?" Astyages asked sourly.

"They'll place us in a wooden tub, only our head will stick out, and then paint our face with milk and honey. Flies will begin to swarm around our nose and eyelids. They didn't let us die but fly's worms will devour our body. Some victims could survive for seventeen days, they decayed alive." He spat bloody phlegm onto the ashes. "I can't even think about it without cringing, every way to die is better than the shit which awaits us."

"So don't think about that right now," Astyages said with the sullen face.

"What you're thinking about? Mithra?!"

"Yes!" Astyages said with an effort. He closed his eyes for a heartbeat and turning to the wall again.

"Don't worry!" Bertkaameh said. "She's going to be right. He will take care of her to achieve his goals."

"He loves her." Astyages could feel his heart fluttering in his chest, "by the expression with which he gazed at her, it was clear that he was praising her." He sneered. "I don't know if I should've been happy or sad."

The door opened with a crash and Hooraan stood in the doorway, looking at them with his narrow almond eyes. It was still dark and quiet, and he had a torch in his hand. Astyages gave his eyes a moment to adjust then looked at him; he recognized bloodstains in his clothes easily enough. Hooran was grimy faced and black handed.

"They say, they say, they're going to kill you in the morning." Hooraan had swollen eyes from crying, he went to Astyages. "You have to come with me! They're going to kill you in the morning!" He said, as he untied Astyages.

"Hooraan, what the fuck are you doing?" Astyages growled. "Get out of here now!"

"They say that they're going to kill you in the morning," he said again, untied Bertkaameh this time.

Astyages reached out and took Hooraan's hand. "I told you to get out of here, now." He caressed Horan's head. "There's nothing you can do, Hooraan. You're playing with fire if the commander finds out... you know him?"

"I'm going to get you out of here!"

Astyages glanced out with an impatient look. "There's no way out."

"It is!" Hooraan said with exasperation contradicted. "There's a magic door."

Bertkaameh grinned as he was rubbing his sore arms.

"My grandfather showed me the magic door," Hooraan said.

"Leave from here, if not I'll be beyond annoyed." Astyages' voice was stiff.

"Wait a minute. Wait!" Bertkaameh said hastily. "Hooraan, can you get us in that thing?"

Hooraan seemed quite pleased with his words. "I do!" He said, nodding.

"What are you talking to him for?" Astyages asked Bertkaameh, shocked. "Have you believe there actually is a magic door?"

"You're going think this is kind of a fucked up because it is," he grinned. "Hooraan's grandfather was a slave, a great builder from Babylon. Great King asked him to design his dream palace."

Astyages was overwhelmed with amazement; Bertkaameh nodded slowly, with a lazy smile.

There was no reason that Astyages could not take him seriously. His face grew serious.

"Let's gamble our fates on him… we have nothing to lose!"

Astyages nodded thinking.

Bertkaameh took Hooraan's hand. "Hooraan, get us out of here."

They stepped out into the darkness. Astyages looked at the soldier dead in front of the door, the rusted nail lodged deep in her throat. The courtyard was hazy with smoke and dust. As their barefoot touches the soil, their toes are bathed in the new waterhole. The rain had stopped and everywhere was silvered and transformed by the light of the full moon, hung like a great luminous pearl on the breast of the sky. They followed Hooraan under cover of darkness, wary of unexpected eyes but the soldiers were too tired to guard the camp all the night, or they never could imagine that someone wanted to run away after subduing the rebels.

Hooraan led them to the west, just in the opposite direction, where they did not want to go. Astyages and Bertkaameh exchanged glances; they were going away from the river. The river was the only point where they could pass the wall that surrounded the city. They reached the iron door that opened on the armory. The doors were open; five men were down, dead. Hooraan hurried on, diagonally, across the big arsenal like a huge hall, full of tackles, levers, ropes, and nails. At the back was an old brick kiln, which no doubt would be left for a few years. Hooraan tried to open its rusted door. Bertkaameh went to help him. He sputtered and struggled. The door opened at last, with a sound like the howling of a beast being slaughtered and their eyes had grown large when they read what had engraved behind the door: You cannot hide magic, not from those who know what to look for.

CHAPTER SEVEN

ETERNAL LOVE

BABYLON, 612 BC, Autumn

Just over the top of a hill, Astyages with his suite came on the patch of licorice. He witnessed from above the Babylon army, formed in columns by divisions, descended, by a simultaneous movement and like one man. Astyages shuddering at his memories as a warm-keen wind blew straight in his face…

*****

The border of Babylon, 626 BC, Autumn

They were running, seeing the long grass fleeing. They went into the reeds. The wet reeds were shimmering like diamond prisms.

"You are slow!" Bertkaameh shouted angrily to Astyages who was running, exhausted with his bare feet over the broken, wet reeds. They eat nothing but roots and locusts for a week and fatigue overcame him for a few minutes, he sat down on a stone. Bertkaameh turned back to him.

"Hang on, man. Hang on!" Bertkaameh said as he pointed out. "Get up. We're nearly my homeland, Babylon!"

Far to the west, in a haze lay the meres; he could see barely steeply pitched roofs of mud houses.

When LORD Bertkaameh, gorgeous in his green Babylon army uniform, accompanied him ceremoniously to the door, Astyages could not believe they were slaves only two weeks before. Bertkaameh saw him on a chestnut mare, his gift to Astyages.

"Nothing to worry," Bertkaameh said. "We'll just go back, an alliance will strengthen us both, Medes and Babylon, and we'll overcome Assyrians." He smiled, excited. "You're just going to have to wait a bit."

Astyages smiled a sad smile and nodded.

Bertkaameh watched him as he galloped away.

"My prayers go with you, my friend," Bertkaameh whispered under his breath.

*****

Babylon, 612 BC, Autumn

"Yes, I just had to wait a bit...," Astyages smiled bitterly, "for seventeen years!" He whispered.

The day Sin-Etli's death was announced, Astyages arrived Hegmataneh. They said it was a heart attack. *Wolf's bane poisoning,* Astyages thought. Everything was all set; Sinshar became king as was predicted. Scythians had an intimate affair with him, the latest step in a dance that went back many years. Scythians attacked Medes with Sinshar support, and Hegmataneh was entirely under their authority for many years. They were bitter years for Medes government, full of misery, hardship, and helplessness.

Now it is over, Astyages thought.

Great Magi, the king's first Minister's defensive strategy didn't have a chivalrous nature but worked! The king of Medes asked all the Scythians commanders to come to his great, luxuriant Medes New Year celebration. They had never imagined that they had walked into a trap, and the king's army was about to attack them. But in the middle of the night, when the Scythians commanders were too drunk to stay in their seats, astonished by the beautiful Median girls' dance, the king left the party, and the attack began in the dark corner of a crowded party. They all were killed there except the leader, who was ready to made peace with the Medes King.

After years, it was the right time to break Assyrians power. Babylon and Medes interested to be more aligned now than they had been in the past seventy years.

Recognition dawned on the Astyages' face. Bertkaameh was coming forward. He had been on horseback, the others following him. Astyages stood before Bertkaameh, seeming now strong and sturdy, unlike the years before.

The change in Bertkaameh's appearance after seventeen years had actually surprised Astyages. He had wings of wiry silver hair sprouting from his temples with wrinkles at the corners of his eyes and a slight increase in weight that suited him.

"So much has changed these past seventeen years!" Bertkaameh said, laughing. He still had all his teeth.

Astyages grinned bitterly in his response. "Yes, years had passed before I knew it," he said. "Man, good to see you, brother."

"Everything is ready for your army settlement," Bertkaameh said. "Let's go to my home. You know, it will be so wonderful to talk to you after all these years."

Astyages saw in Bertkaameh's house his impressionable, smiling kids' faces smiling at their own happiness, feeling the eager bustle around him. Bertkaameh's beautiful wife was carrying their dinner on a tray. "I waited for the servants to pull the fresh loaves from the ovens, my Lord. The bread's still hot."

Bertkaameh took the tray from her hand, smiling, and she left them alone.

"It looks like you fulfill a dream of a good life through hard work and bravery," Astyages said to Bertkaameh.

"A damn good, really good life my friend!" Bertkaameh glanced at Astyages as he uncovered platters. Under the lid, he discovered a blood beef stew, golden brown and crispy fried chicken. "But you're making the 'I'm not good at life' face," he said, laughing, "so, tell me, have you married yet?"

Astyages nodded, thoughtfully. "I am married to a Lydian[1] woman," he said as he tore off a bit of bread, "a marriage in kindled hope to unite two Lydian and Medes kingdom as one!" *A forced marriage, just for unity, as many as marriages in the court,* Astyages thought. "I have two children, a son, and a daughter." He smiled, a sad smile. "I love my daughter."

---

[1] Lydia was an Iron Age kingdom of western Asia Minor located generally east of ancient Ionia in the modern western Turkey.

Bertkaameh stared at his friend; his eyes were full of nothing but sorrow.

"I've heard so many things about her... new Semiramis." Bertkaameh said cautiously.

"Yeah...," Astyages said without removing his eyes from the bread, "... people say, she is Assyria's beloved sovereign queen." He raised his head slowly and stared at Bertkaameh's eyes. "They say, with new Semiramis' love, King Sinshar's power is unbroken and eternal." He dropped the spoon.

"Myth and mystery...," Bertkaameh said. "Who better than you knows the truth?"

Astyages shook his head. "I don't know my friend, I really don't know!" He stared at him. "Seventeen years ago I just wanted to get back there and save her but many years has slipped by... that's all changed, everything's changed."

"Were you at all able to forget things and enjoy your life?"

Astyages sighed. "Believe me, I wish I could," he said. "I've been waiting my whole life for today, but I'm afraid now. I can fight the whole world... but not with her."

"Your king leave you no choice. You know better than me, the king of Medes has laid siege to the city of Ashur. It took him six months to starve them out. You would need to be ready my friend, we'll get one day, maybe two, then we could storm Ashur, and the city would fall, not long after the fall of this city, it'll be Nineveh's turn soon," Bertkaameh said, his eyes fixed on Astyages' face, sullenly.

"I know my king's order is strict and must be put into execution this instant," Astyages said, irritated.

Bertkaameh took a deep breath. "Fine. We've become the commanders of the combined army of Babylon and Medes, so we can't come back empty handed," he glanced at blissful vacancy on his friend's face. "We can help each other to make a better fate for others."

Astyages nodded but did not seem to get better. "Maybe, this is what fate desires," he said.

*****

Nineveh, 612 BC, Autumn

Slowly, her beautiful golden honey eyes ran over the people.

There was still a crowd on the forte's yard. It had been Assyrians habit, ever since the famine. The people came pouring down from everywhere, on a horse, on a camel, and on foot, to talk to their Queen. New Semiramis was willing to provide her people's needs.

She looked with penetrating eyes at a woman, who stood pale and trembling, a baby in her arms. "Come forward," Mithra said, wiping the sweat from her brow with an embroidered handkerchief as she thought she had never been used to Nineveh's hot and humid weather.

The woman bowed, the baby moaned into the blanket that covered her. Mithra smiled and reached out a hand to stroke her cheek. The baby sneezed, and Mithra laughed unconsciously but then something indefinable, something like a pain, made her feel suddenly miserable. Mithra did not know she should appreciate the labor camp commander's sword hit that caused she never have a baby with Sinshar or curse him because she never could be a mother.

Mithra slowly withdrew her hand. The woman was waited in silence, bowing her head

"What's your problem?"

She bowed again. "I'm begging you, Your Highness," She looked uncomfortable. "Her father's dead... at war and I can't afford to live and take care of my child alone."

"They commonly give the soldiers a good fixed income!" Mithra said, frowning.

"Yes, but they told me only alive soldiers entitled to the fund." She fell silent, frightened.

Mithra took a deep breath to calm herself. As far back as she could remember, Sinshar had always been the same, he still accepted what Mithra wanted, then he became penitent, as he always did on serious occasions.

Mithra beckoned to a soldier who stood beside her. "Give her twenty silver coins." She made herself smile. "I'll take care of you. Don't worry; you'll be coming here every other month to receive your stipend."

The young woman's anxiety faded, and a tremulous smile crept across her face. She bowed again and made to go.

"That's enough for today!" Mithra said as she got up. Her voice was heard under the sound of her silk dress rustling around her.

She had put on a warm yellow silk dress coming only halfway down her calves, with loose elbow sleeves, no waist, her initials embroidered over the heart, appropriate to the rites of autumn. Her dark red hair was more wild in Nineveh's humid days, and she had to have a maid to tame her impossibly curly hair. Sinshar had faith that Mithra's heart would soften with old age but seemed age was unable to diminish her beauty as well as her stubbornness.

The guards were keeping the crowds away, closing the forte's front door.

"Your Majesty... Your Majesty..."

From the corner of her eye, Mithra saw fellow shoved men aside to open a way through the crowd.

"If Your Majesty will hear my words..."

The soldiers were trying to stop him from getting in. His simple sleeveless garment was evidently a mark that this man assisted the priests at the temple.

"God has a VERY important message for you...," the man shouted.

Somewhere a crow cawed with bold assurance.

"Let him come in!" Mithra said, her heart thumped in fear.

The soldiers made way for the man. He came forward and knelt, head bowed.

"Well, tell me your important message!" Mithra said.

"The high priest asked me to give a message to you... Your Majesty," he said with an awkward diffidence voice. "God says I will make an end of it. Affliction will not rise up a second time. They shall be devoured like stubble fully dried. Though they are safe, and likewise many, yet in this manner, they will be cut down when he passes through. The gates of your land are wide open to your enemies; fire has consumed the bars of your gates. There the fire will consume you; the sword will cut you down. They will

194

devour you like a swarm of locusts. Multiply like grasshoppers, multiply like locusts! King of Assyria, your shepherd's slumber; your nobles lie down to rest. Your people are scattered on the mountains with no one to gather them. Nothing can heal you; your wound is fatal."

When the man ceased speaking, all were gazing spitefully at him. His word was a dagger in her heart, Mithra stared at him, trembling, listening to the muffled stillness broken only by the cawing of crows.

One of the soldiers grabbed him by the throat and shoved him back against the barracks wall. "Shout your mouth, you stinking rogue!" The soldier cried fiercely to his.

"Leave him!" Mithra cried roughly.

The man's words were ringing in her ears yet. Hearing those words after years… seemed inconceivable, incredible, impossible!

Mithra got up, trying to control the trembling of her knees. "Gave him some gold coins," she said quietly to her guard, standing beside her.

"But Your Majesty…"

"Did not you hear what I just said?!" Mithra said sharply.

"Right away, my Queen."

Mithra stepped toward her carriage; she glanced back as she reached the door. "Say your high priest, I'm obliged to him for this message but… maybe, this is what fate desires."

*****

195

Her footsteps sent soft echoes hurrying ahead of her as leaped over the stone steps, in Yaafa's colossal palace. For seventeen years, this palace had been the only place that she could name it home. She had been living only a few months at the king's palace, and then return her aunt's home, with the pretext of caring for Yaafa, who had become severely ill. Mithra found it more and more agreeable to be with Yaafa, seeing her un-healed- stinking wounds, hearing her wailing, she could not stand hearing Sinshar's midnight amorous deliriums and his growing jealous.

Yaafa, only a year later, had died; her last days were indeed filled with woe and pain but full of kindness at the same time. Mithra strangely was beginning to understand how much she really loved Yaafa, a woman that one day she hated most. Maybe it was because now there was no one in Yaafa's life but Mithra or that Mithra had learned to see imperceptible others soul, and saw distinctly that they were all good at heart.

"Pardon, my Queen, Lord Mahbod insists..."

Mithra heard her maid's voice from behind. She turned her head and blinked at her brother, following the maid. Mahbod gave her his brightest smile. He had changed considerably in years, his skin looked as pale leather, with a forked beard, and strangely he seemed even taller and stouter and his arm, strong and muscular, was bare to the elbow. Everything had changed in his but his attitude.

Mahbod stepped forward gracefully in his army green uniform, removed his hat, and bowed. "My Queen!"

Mithra managed a weak little smile. "My dear brother!" They had learned that they had to act in front of others. "You have come a long way, and rest and refreshment would be most welcome.

196

Might we continue on to the private sitting room?" The queen's voice was soft as silk.

"Willingly, Your Majesty," said Mahbod.

At the top of the stairs, a door stood ajar to her left. Mithra knew Hara was peeking through the door. They entered the private sitting room, the door closed.

"What the fuck are you doing again?" Mithra said immediately. "You should know, I haven't seen Sinshar in months, and I don't expect to, so I cannot want anything from him."

"That is kind of you." Mahbod laughed. "Even if you have not seen him for years, I'm sure the king will listen to you... but that's not why I really came."

"So why'd you come to see me?" Mithra said dryly as she filled two purple wine cups and offered it to Mahbod.

He took it, drank immediately. "I want to talk about something important."

Mithra sipped daintily at her wine. "Say what you came to say."

"Medes' troops have conquered the city of Ashur and Nineveh will be under siege very soon!" Mahbod said in a voice strangely flat and emotionless.

Mithra could feel the cup shaking in her hand. "How do you know? I haven't heard anything about it!" She said.

"Well, Sinshar has tried very hard to hide it, but I just heard it from Saber."

"Saber?" Mithra said and laughed, sourly. "How would Saber so know? He's not coming out of his house even."

"Saber has his spies everywhere," Mahbod said, smiling.

Mithra filled her wine cup again, wanting nothing so much as to pour the cup over his head and drown his sly smile. "As of right now, no one has found a good way to get past Nineveh's wall!" She said thoughtfully.

"The king of Medes comes against the Nineveh in a war with Babylon army and has taken their provisions and their weapons of war."

God says I will make an end of it, Mithra remembered the man's word with her last sip of wine.

"What will you do?"

Mithra looked at him, perplexed. "What shall I do?"

Mahbod smiled. "Well, your prince is leading the Medes army… you can still save yourself. Do you want to give him a message?"

"How can you live such a hellish existence?" Mithra said in a disgusted tone. She turned her face, stared into the distance and sighed. "I couldn't betray this people confidence. I'll wait, and I'll do what is best for us, for people." She turned back to Mahbod. "Well, I heard you, now, leave."

"You're absolutely right. I've finished!" said Mahbod, getting up. He went to the door.

When Mahbod came to the hall, he found Hara waiting for him at the top of the steps.

"You promised… You promised you will come every day to meet me…," Hara said staring at him.

Mahbod passed her negligently, but every time she met him, there surged up in her heart that same feeling of quickened life that had come upon her that day in the ceremony when she saw him for the first time.

"Why didn't you come?" Hara cried as she grabbed hold of him. "Don't leave me... don't leave me!"

"Leave me alone!" Mahbod said cruelly as he wrenched free of her.

The servants from the Hall, constantly craning necks, took a quick peek. Mithra went over and put a comforting arm around her. "Hara... let him go!"

Hara wept and looked at Mithra; her eyes were red and miserable.

"Why don't you get it? He's not Armaz; he doesn't deserve your love." Mithra whispered in Hara's ear as she took her to her room.

Hara stopped short in the doorway and gazed on Mithra, unconscious of everything. "You... you are to blame for everything!" she cried, with tears of despair and hatred in her voice. She looked like a crazy person, with flying gray hair and bloodshot eyes.

"I didn't do nothing!" Mithra said.

Hara wrenched herself free. "Yes, you hate me..." Her words broke up in a fit of coughing. "All you have ever done is fuck up my life!" She said in a meek voice, though she was angry enough to spit.

Mithra looked at her with concern. "I didn't do nothing!" She said again in the kind, quiet tone, trying to be pleasant to her perturbed spirit. "I'll give you some hot wine with cloves, just calm down and stop making your cough worse." Mithra turned the handle, pushed the door open and gently led her into the room. She covered her with a blanket and sat at the bedside listening to her uneven breathing. A few minutes later, the only sound was her faint soft sobbing. Mithra gently stroked her hair.

She found it difficult to hate anyone for long when she looked at Hara!

*****

Sinshar took the letter, dismissed the soldier with a wave and cracked the seal. He shuffled through the letters slowly, reading each one over several times. His face was twisted with anger to the likeness of a wild beast, lost in his thoughts. He no longer seemed stout, though he still had the appearance of solidity and strength hereditary in his family. His round belly and the bags under his eyes showed the countless evening feasts and drinking too much wine.

News has been coming upriver, none of it good, Sinshar thought.

There were increasing rebellions in Great Assyria, and a big part of his army was suppressing them in the different regions. A famine had sent hundreds to their grave and their farms had trouble because of the drought. The Marduk's prophets had implored their god to end the drought afflicting the land. *Marduk had proved unable to do so,* Sinshar thought. The people misery and complaints will take this situation to the worse. In between, since Arsen's death, there were not many in the court who supported him. The throne rests on an illegitimate bastard; it was whispered in a conspiracy.

Sinshar leaned back in his chair. He had demanded assistance at Scythians as usual, but this letter, which he received now, showed him Scythians had refused to help Assyria.

Sinshar did not know the game, and the king of Medes had beaten him easily.

"Your Majesty." His guard stood in the door, a taper in his hand. "Lord Mahbod has come. You asked to be told."

"Show him in," the king said.

The guard held the door and gestured Mahbod through.

"My King," Mahbod said, his face bright with a cringing smile, "May I sit? "

Mahbod's company was the last thing Sinshar would have wanted, but the king said. "A chair for Lord."

"May I offer you refreshment?" The guard asked.

"No need," The king's cold voice rang through space. "Have there been any further tidings of our sweet queen?" The king said to Mahbod, as soon as they were left alone.

"There's no way Mithra betray you!" Mahbod proudly proclaimed.

"Look, I'm not asking for your opinion, tell me exactly what she said," Sinshar said, his voice was thick and angry.

Mahbod looked at the king and became afraid. "She said, I couldn't betray this people confidence, and I'll do what is best for the people."

Mahbod was waiting in an agony of fear, but the king took little notice of his presence, looking thoughtful. All that she had said, with the earnestness of sincerity was not what pleases the king. Sinshar preferred she had said she would never betray his husband. *Who knows what is best for the people,* Sinshar thought.

"There can be no danger, surely?"

Mahbod's fearful voice brought Sinshar to his sense. The king frowned at him and rattled the parchment angrily. "Nineveh doesn't fail, never!"

Mahbod nodded vigorously as if he had taken his words to heart. "Saber..."

"Look," the king interrupted. "You must keep him quiet!" He said imperiously.

Mahbod shrugged a little uneasily. "Nobody cares what he says."

"So no-one cares whether he lives or die!" The king said quietly.

Mahbod nodded. "I do whatever pleases you, my King," he said.

"The sooner, the better," Sinshar said. "All right, Lord Mahbod, you can go."

The king's voice lingered over the word 'Lord', and this sounded pleasant to Mahbod. He got up, bowed and went. His footsteps echoed through the vault as he made his way between the rows of pillars, smiling.

Not Hara, not Saber, was no longer working for him so well but now, the king's strength offers him a so safe prop.

*****

Saber's mouth was full of blood. He spat it into the basin and took a soft damp cloth, laid it across his mouth as he eased himself into his bench. The blood came before the pain, and he gritted his teeth against the excruciating pain. He lay there waiting for the waves of burning pain in his stomach to recede, then he tried to draw a breath. Everything he put down, he just was throwing up, and Saber grew quite used to see fresh blood when he vomited. As he could not lift the jug, he tipped it over painfully towards his mouth and swallowed a draught.

I'm at the gates of death, Saber thought, *I don't cling to life sufficiently to fear death!* This was true, but sometimes he was suddenly overcome by fear not only of death but also of sickness and weakness, and involuntarily he scrutinized his bare arm, surprised at its thinness. That was like a new being born within him, tearing his stomach strings, torturing him. He could hear its ticking all day long, the crunch of chewing his stomach and his intestines.

He was so busy with his bitter thoughts that he heard knocking on the door after two or three times.

"What do you want?" Saber shouted.

"Lord Mahbod has come," his servant said behind the door, he knew nobody was allowed to enter Saber's room. Saber did not want anyone to know of his illness.

"Show him the guest chamber, I'll join him there."

Saber found Mahbod beside the window, gazed out, frowning. He hesitated for a few moments, long enough to enjoy his profile. He smiled, then gasped as pain flared in his stomach.

"You mean you come all this way to see me?" Saber said.

Mahbod turned to him, gave him a slow, cold smile. "I've missed you so much, Saber!" He said, but his blank expression didn't show his words.

"It's great," Saber said as he went toward him, hoping his pain grew less acute in his presence. "Nothing delights me so much as being with you." He sat on a bench of polished ebony, covered with the cushions that made him more comfortable and put a hand on Mahbod's arm. "How long till you are ready to go? We don't have much time. You needed to get out of the fight."

Mahbod looked at him nervously, one foot jiggling with impatience.

"Look, you'll have to get out of here, sonny..."

Mahbod interrupted. "Nineveh doesn't fail, never!"

"Don't be silly," Saber said, impatiently. "We can't fight them."

"Please don't be afraid... nothing happens, and there is always room for my growth," Mahbod said.

His voice still held a remnant of calmness, but beneath his words, Saber could feel coldness fighting its way to the surface, coldness as cruel as the crack of a whip. He knew this coldness. His memory made it hard to breathe...

*****

HEGMATANEH, The land of MEDIA, 649BC, Winter

"Come on, son, what do you say?"

Snow was flying as they were riding through the woods on the side of the river. Saber was of twenty, thin as a dry stick. He was ambitious, egotistical and obsessed with proud. On the way home, his father talked a lot of drunken nonsense to him, like always. Saber swung slowly with the motion of his horse, busy with his own thoughts.

"Didn't you hear a goddamn word I said?" His father said.

Saber turned to him, his father, big, erect, with his snow-white hair and beard, leaning upon his saddle horn, and stared at him. He looked nothing like his father. *I don't believe he is really my father,* Saber thought.

"What did you say? I didn't hear you!" Saber said as he stared at the road again. He was familiar with this road, he had explored every inch of the region, even the riverbed; he knew the forest from one tree to another.

"Man, didn't you hear that shit?" His father said. "I want to take one of those stupid men down."

"I joy in my own success alone," Saber said.

"What's mine is yours!" His father said, laughing.

Snow was falling still. Heavy, silent, like Saber.

"What the hell is wrong with you?" His father shouted, impatiently. "Speak, you piece of shit."

Saber glanced at him. "I'm somewhat worried. Someone's in my way," he said calmly.

"Who?"

"You!" He said.

"I'm not in your way, goddamn son of a bitch; I'm going to make way for you!"

Saber silently studied him for what seemed to his father to be an eternity. "I have learned from you never to trust anyone," he said as he put his dagger in his father's horseback.

So suddenly, the mare started, gave a frightened whinny and raced off through the frozen muddy road at a gallop. All was going according to Saber's plan. The horse raced through the trees, regardless of his father last effort to calm her down. Looking ahead, he could see only tree trunks of innumerable sizes and shapes: straight or bent, squat or slender; all green with moss, just a little in advance, a gnarled branch collided with the side of his head, swept him out of his saddle, and he dropped violently to the ground. The mare went past with trailing bridle and empty saddle.

"Dear father, I just learned that life is short and crappy, and you have to take what you can, while you can!" Saber said.

*****

Nineveh, 612 BC, Autumn

"I want to join the Assyrian army and be as successful as you."

Saber nodded, his sad eyes lingered on Mahbod's eyes for three long heartbeats. His eyes were like two pristine stones of onyx that lit up with a purple flare when touched by candlelight.

"Are you going to throw me over?!" Saber said, calmly.

"I should learn how to be my own man," Mahbod said. He stared, and Saber sitting against him stared back. "Forgive me, if I don't do this, somebody else will, but at least the king will give me a role in the court."

The sudden spasm of pain made Saber's hand tighten. His nails dug into the cushions. He smiled. "Now, as long as you and I are alone, why don't you tell me exactly what's on your mind?"

"I don't want to see you get hurt," Mahbod said as he fumbled in his pocket, drew out a small bottle, and opened it.

Belladonna poisoning, no one expected anything better from Mahbod. Well, he was never as smart or as brave as his sister was! Saber thought. "So let toast to you, sonny."

Mahbod bolted the contents with one abrupt motion of his arm and Saber seized it greedily and drank it out.

Death is not the scariest thing in life. The scariest thing is what dies inside us while we live, Saber thought in his final moment.

*****

"I am not your prisoner, Sinshar," Mithra shouted angrily. "Open the doors and let me go!"

"Prisoner? You're my queen, and I'm your king, and this palace is your home!" Sinshar said as he turned his head away and gazed out across high above the hill, where so many slaves had previously perished from thirst and hard work once, and now an attractive garden was made there. The garden stretched up into town, the palm trees were the jewels in the garden, with the waterfalls between the ponds. Sinshar's eyes could not see the charms of the garden. He stared anxiously at the wall opposite him, where was heard the din of arms, with the crying of men and the neighing of horses.

"You can't keep me here!"

Mithra's angry voice brought Sinshar to his sense.

"You can hide in your palace, but I'm going... people were terrified, they need me."

"They need not fear." Sinshar gave her a long look. "Nineveh doesn't fell, never! God Marduk will protect his people."

Mithra grinned. "Such a beautiful quote," Mithra said. "I could feel our Marduk God's gaze upon us... I've heard the Medes army has burned all Marduk's statues. He has saved himself if he could."

"Bullshit! It's better to keep your mouth shut, the queen of Assyria!" Sinshar said with a stupid mixture of ridicule and rage.

"Why are you so worried then if you think it's bullshit?" Mithra said.

"You're all I have in the world, and you're the only one who drives me crazy," Sinshar roared.

"Just the opposite! I'm the only one who speaks the truth to bring you to your senses." She moved from her chair and went in front of him, in front of the window, saying, "The time of great Assyria was over. No kingdom with a desire to kill, to torture, to smash faces in with a sledgehammer, won't be alive for long. You have to surrender to this current, and use its power as your own."

Sinshar's left eyelid fluttering furiously, his mouth twisted up in a moue of distaste, "Just stop saying that, or…"

Mithra might have said more, but suddenly her eyes gaped wide without paying any more attention to Sinshar. He followed her gaze and saw Nineveh's great wall came tumbling down.

*****

The wind was gusting, around the hooves of their horses. All the Medes' warriors wore red, with the vest of lion's fur, and conical bronze helms topped with a sharpened spike. They stood stiffly at attention, their eyes fixed straight ahead. It was a fantastic moment.

Cyaxares, the king of Medes, in a plain red uniform, his gold helmet beneath one arm, on his shaggy grey horse, stared at the wall opposite him. His groomed mustache was silver-white, his broad forehead had numerous lines, his eyes shining, the look upon his face was lustful… the great Nineveh's wall was breaking up before his eyes, like a mountain crumbling.

Astyages stood beside him, tall and fair, his helmet dark bronze, yet he looked more regal in bronze than the king did in gold. His eyes were dark brown and fearless, unflinching. His dark hair had been done up in a thick braid. He kept looking straight ahead, his face showed no emotion. For him, the Nineveh's wall breaking up was easy to believe, he had lived this moment again and again and again when he was a slave in Nineveh. The Nineveh's wall was high, giants and colossal but was made of sun-dried bricks. The Medes army had made camp outside the wall and set to building catapults and siege engines. They were dumping huge stones in the river for more than two months, down pouring of rocks caused the overflowing Tigris River. The waters upstream rose up like a dam an allowed the waters downstream to the

Nineveh's wall. That could able to weaken the huge pile of bricks then Astyages ordered them flung from the walls with catapults. Only in minutes, dust seeped from the rough wall and collapsed. For minutes, the dust continued to fly from the wall, it looked as though a greyish haze of dust hung thin and motionless against the sun, but gradually, the strong east wind drove the dust back.

Nineveh showed itself, naked, defenseless.

Nabopolassar, the king of Babylon, with arms hanging down and with a puckered, frowned face, approached on horseback beside Cyaxares with a gracefully majestic. He was not as happy as Cyaxares, though this was a great win for him, he believed in God Marduk too, and this triumph was for a false religion, which could be generally undesirable.

You give me no choice, Sinshar! Nabopolassar thought.

Such awful bad luck face maybe won't get us to the end of this, Astyages thought, glancing at the king of Babylon's stern, serious face. He rubbed his high forehead, as though to drive away something and looked away, to Cyaxares' face.

"Inspect our weapons and put the men on alert," Cyaxares roared. His voice was thunder.

The red men were ready. They had broad shoulders, a red face, a crushing fist, a bold heart, a loyal soul, and a sincere, terrible eye. The great masses of crumbling stone had fallen inward the city and heaped against the wall. The wooden rafts took men quickly towards Nineveh. They recognized the headlong sounds of the Assyrian soldiers towards the crumbling wall on the city side. The Assyrians seemed bewildered.

"The time to strike," Astyages whispered.

The king of Medes, oblivious to Nabopolassar raised his hand. A stout husky man, with a horn to mouth, stood up in his saddle. The king put down his hand, the horn's voice was heard and...

The men's great roar rose up as if it was the end of the world.

*****

The battle for the palace was on, though five miles away from the palace, but was so loud as to seem almost in the next street. The Assyrians' soldiers were amazed at the Medes warriors' boldness, feared every minute to be surrounded and captured by them, and hid in the forte. The sound of wheels and footsteps was heard almost everywhere, in a tone which made the men shudder. Nineveh was full of frightened people. The Lord Commander own men were struggling into armor. He looked on their fearful faces, whispering to one another.

The king of the Medes knew well the Assyrian warrior were faster and stronger and that was why he had trained highly skilled archers who had the huge bows which they used better than anyone else in the world and could hit a small bird into the air let alone the Assyrians frightened, frantic soldiers.

The labor's camp lord commander was looking at the city from the wooden watchtower. The city stank of blood and fear, he was war hardened enough to know they will have failed.

"We have war inside the city too," the senior commander said when he saw the corpses on the ground. "I warned you that this day would come, my Lord!"

The lord commander turned to him, his face was awful in anger and wretchedness, he grabbed his senior commander by the collar. "Where's this clown?"

"Who, my Lord?" The senior commander mumbled, his eyes narrowed against the lord commander terrible bright eyes.

"Who has bestowed the name of a king to himself," the lord commander said through gritted teeth.

"No one seems to know what happened to him!" The senior commander, trembling.

"There's nothing to wait," the lord commander said as he released him. Taking a run, he dashed down the steps, whispering curses. "Bring me a God Marduk's altar!" He shouted in the courtyard.

The senior commander could only gape in a sort of dull bewilderment.

"Didn't you hear me?" The lord commander said. "Find an altar with God Marduk's statue on it."

The senior commander went wandering up the street.

"Bring some heads too, children and women!"

The senior commander heard the lord commander's voice from behind and stopped once more. "Where shall I get the child from?" He said, "There's no child or woman amongst the enemies!"

"Are you fucking crazy?" The lord commander said, his boils were red with rage. "I need goddamned the Assyrians children and women's heads."

The senior commander was overwhelmed with wonder. "Where will I get them??"

"This city is filled with the dead. Behead some corpses; if you don't find any, behead some alive…," said the lord commander, taking a step toward him. "Otherwise I beheaded your young wife and her children."

The senior commander took a hasty step backward as he nodded. Only one hour later, the altar was in front of the lord commander. A white, silk veil hung behind the altar, on God Marduk's statue, covered with blood. Some children's heads, with staring eyes and open mouth, had completed this frightening image.

"It's worse than I feared," the lord commander said while he stroked his beard with satisfaction. "Put it in a cart and ride around the city…" He turned to the soldiers who stood bewildered there. "You should march around the city, don't fight anyone, just shout out this: the blood was shed on the God Marduk's altar. He will express his vengeance and proves his sovereignty."

*****

Sinshar's hand had grabbed her arm, his five fingers hard as iron digging deep into her flesh.

"Come with me. Hurry!" Sinshar roared, his breath foul with the smell of wine. Their boots sank into pools of steaming oil that Sinshar was poring on the floor. He ran as quickly as he could, oblivious to Mithra's struggling. Mithra was fighting with him in every step as she took three steps to every stride of Sinshar's boots.

The jar of oil was more than half empty; Sinshar put it hastily away and snatched up a torch from the sconces along the walls. He gave his beautiful palace one last lingering look, reached out his hand, and the curtains, drenched with oil got on fire. Mithra could hear every person in the harem, the women and eunuchs, screaming as they ran to the door, and saw the play of light against the marbles, reflections of the fires.

The flames had spread around the palace.

Sinshar stared at the fire for a long time. He hauled Mithra, still struggling, and dragged her through the long the main hallway. At the end of the hall, they entered the king's private room. Sinshar stood in front of a precious red carpet and angrily pulling down the rug. A dark passage was waiting for them behind the carpet. The corridor was lit by no shaft and was utterly dark; he took a torch and walked quickly to the hallway.

Mithra was bending her head down, as her right hand tightly clenched upon the edge of the door. "Goddammit! Where are you taking me?"

He hit her. It was a slap, backhanded, but he put all his strength into it, all his rage. Mithra was squatting, unbalanced. The blow sent her tumbling backward to the floor, but he caught her as she fell, neatly. He was walking through the winding stone steps to the crypts beneath the palace, hurried and preoccupied, in his soft boots. He was breathing heavily by the time they reached the bottom of the stairs, his face red in the torchlight as he stepped out into the darkness of the crypt. Sinshar put Mithra gently on a bed of the most precious silk carpets and lit other torches. The shadows moved and lurched. The flickering light touched the stones underfoot and brushed against the granite pillars. Mithra could see a great load of treasure, things of gold, silver, copper, and bronze; many beads and chains and jeweled ornaments.

"Why would you want to go down to the crypts?" Mithra said. "Your soldiers are fighting hard to save this land, and you just hide here."

"I did not hide!" Sinshar roared, furious.

Mithra gave him a sour grin. "Then, why are you here?" She said.

Sinshar squatted in front of her and moved the torch close. "The Assyrian people bury their kings with all his precious possessions, do you know why?"

Mithra had never seen him like this before, in delirium and weakness and she was a little frightened. Mithra looked with an aspect of great perplexity into his face, powerless to answer but Sinshar expected no response, and he started to speak without giving her time to reply. "We will open our eyes in the otherworld, in God Marduk kingdom, with all we need around us." He silently fixed his eyes on Mithra for long moments. "I just want to be with you, wherever that is."

"I don't believe even your God Marduk wants a coward king in his presence who has abandoned his people," she said disgustedly.

Sinshar's mouth twisted in a fury, squeezed the torch harder. For a long moment, the only sound was the king grinding his teeth. "Damn you!" He shouted as he got up slowly.

He stepped forward, clutching the torch with both hands. He swung it about his head in a circle, fanning the flames. "You had not stopped thinking of him for a single moment. Am I right? Every time I touch you… you see him instead of me." Sinshar slid the torch on precious, and unique King's robe. In a moment, silk robes caught fire. "The idea of being a stranger in your mind when we have made love make me sick," he shouted louder than ever.

Sinshar continued along the hall away from Mithra and thrust the torch into the rug's pile. A few wisps of smoke began to rise, "So here he is now, back in Nineveh where you live," The first flames appeared, dancing from the ground on up, "but you're mine my Queen; you can never be together because you're coming with me." In moments, a strong carved wooden pillar was engulfed in fire.

"How could I love a man who doesn't even like himself?"

Sinshar could hear her voice just behind, he turned.

Mithra loomed up before him, swinging a torch with both hands as she howled in wordless fury and smashed him hard. Sinshar collapsed to the floor and fall heavily with his face to the ground.

"I lived with you...," Mithra said, with gnashing impetuosity, "... but I never die with you."

She took the stairs, two at a time, her scarlet skirts swishing over the steps. Every few steps she looked back to make certain Sinshar was not coming after her. As she stepped out into the hall, stared wide-eyed at the fires. The stones were cracking and splitting and part of the marble pillar fell away and landed with a crash that shook her. Mithra started running as fast as she could toward the staircase, her ruffled skirt raised to keep it from dragging on the floor. The heat of the flames beat against her face. As the fresh air rushed in through the palace, the fire surged upward. Somewhere a crow cawed with bold assurance; she noticed her skirt was burning. Mithra bent, tried to stifle it with her hands, at that moment a burning Agar pillar collapsed in front of her. Mithra swayed and sank back.

If I had taken only one more step... she thought, panting and wild-eyed. There was no way to the staircase anymore.

Mithra glanced nervously around and retreated towards her own chamber. She went into her room. This was the most significant and airiest in the palace, and it had an interior terrace where it was pleasant to sit at night because of the river breeze and the scent of the rosebushes. She wondered if it would be hard to climb out that terrace. She bolted to the terrace and looked out. The air was filled with dust and smoke, and Nineveh had become a battleground. She was surprised to see, contrary to what Sinshar had imagined, the Medes soldiers did not seem to have the advantage. The Babylon troops were retreating! The Medes army, frightened and sullen, stared at them and the Assyrians warriors were attacking them. The King of Medes had so many men, and he could throw fresh attackers out, but his men were retreating with fear.

The victory was near for Assyrians!